Enid

The Wishing Jug

...and other stories

Bounty
Books

Published in 2015 by Bounty Books,
a division of Octopus Publishing Group Ltd,
Carmelite House
50 Victoria Embankment,
London EC4Y 0DZ
www.octopusbooks.co.uk

An Hachette UK Company
www.hachette.co.uk
Enid Blyton ® Text copyright © 2011 Chorion Rights Ltd.
Illustrations copyright © 2015 Award Publications Ltd.
Layout copyright © 2015 Octopus Publishing Group Ltd.

Illustrated by Dorothy Hamilton.

ISBN: 978-0-75373-049-2

A CIP catalogue record for this book is available from the
British Library.

Printed and bound by CPI Group (UK) Ltd, Croydon, CR0 4YY

CONTENTS

The Wishing Jug   5
Bushy's Secret   30
The Wrong Lunch-Time   36
The Goblin's Dog   44
Mary Brown and Mary Contrary   59
Treacle-Pudding Town   72
Heyho and the North Wind   86
The Dancing Fox-Kettle   103
A Surprising Afternoon   117
The Galloping Seahorse   134
A Hole in Santa's Sack   144
Mr Dear-Me's Handkerchief   153
The Runaway Hat   161
Belinda All Alone   169
Come Back, Dobbin!   180

The Wishing Jug

There was once a poor boy called Tuppeny, who lived with his mother and father in a little tumbledown cottage in the village of Trim. He was a lazy fellow, and, instead of doing his work well, he would dream all day long of what he would do if he were a prince instead of a peasant-boy.

"How fine to live in a castle and have many horses and men of my own," he thought. "I should marry a princess and sit on a throne."

His work was scaring birds away from the fields. He thought so much about what he would do if he were a prince that often the birds came and ate the crops under his very nose. Then his master would be very angry with him.

One day, as he sat there twirling his rattle idly in his hands, quite forgetting to shake it at the greedy birds, he talked aloud to himself.

"I should like to wear a red and gold cloak and hang a glittering sword by my side. I should like a feathered cap, and –"

"Well, and why shouldn't you?" said a voice behind him. Tuppeny looked round. He saw behind him a tall thin man dressed in a cloak with suns, moons and stars all over it. On his head was a pointed hat, and as soon as Tuppeny saw him he knew that he was a wizard. He jumped up and bowed.

"Have you come to ask me to do anything for you?" he said.

"Well," said the wizard, "you might be able to help me out of a difficulty. I have lost the key of my cottage on the hill, and I very much want to get something out of it. I believe you could just squeeze in through a little window that has been left open."

"What will you give me if I do?" asked Tuppeny.

"You shall have the cloak, cap and sword you were wishing for just now!" said the wizard.

"Ho!" said Tuppeny, jumping up and down in delight. "Lead the way, wizard.

I'll climb in through the window for you!"

The wizard led Tuppeny across many
fields and at last came to a steep hill.
Nestling in the side of it, quite hidden
by a clump of trees, was a strange little
cottage. Tuppeny had never seen it before
– indeed he never remembered seeing the
hill either, and puzzled his brains to think
how it was that he had missed it.

They came up to the cottage and
Tuppeny saw that all the curtains were
drawn tightly across the windows. The
gate was locked and they had to climb over
it. The wizard led the way to where a tiny
window at the back had been left open. It

was high up, and Tuppeny wondered how he could reach it.

"I'll climb up this pear-tree," he said. "I think I can just swing myself down to the windowsill if I climb along that branch."

He swung himself up into the tree and climbed along the branch towards the window. Then in a trice he was on the sill, squeezing his body through the opening.

"Shall I open the front door for you?" he asked the wizard. " Then you can come in and get what you want."

"Oh no, don't bother to do that," said the wizard. "All I want is a little red jug you will find in the kitchen in the middle of the table. Just bring me that, there's a good lad."

Tuppeny ran downstairs into the kitchen. On the table was a little red jug with a carved handle. He picked it up – and then he heard a strange noise from outside. He went to the window and looked out. The wizard was fighting a fierce little gnome!

"What are you doing near my cottage?" cried the gnome, furiously. "You've come to steal something, I know you have! It's

a good thing I locked all my doors. Take that, and that, and that!" shouted the gnome, slapping the wizard hard.

The wizard suddenly cried out a strange word, and the gnome disappeared and in his place there came a little whining dog that ran round and round the garden in despair.

Tuppeny was frightened. So this wasn't the wizard's cottage after all! The wizard had sent him to steal the jug. What a

wicked man! Tuppeny was quite sure he wouldn't get the cloak and sword he had been promised, and he began to be afraid that the angry wizard would turn him into something too.

So he stole to the back door, slipped back the bolt that fastened it, and crept out. He ran to a thick bush and crouched underneath. Soon the wizard went to the window and called him.

"Hurry up, boy!" he shouted. "Can't you find the jug?"

When he heard no reply he became angry and shouted more loudly. Suddenly the little gnome-dog ran up and bit him on the leg, and the wizard gave a scream and fled away down the hill. The gnome-dog

10

ran after him, and Tuppeny was left alone
under his bush, trembling.

Soon he crept out and ran home as fast
as his legs would carry him. When he got
there he found that he was carrying the
little red jug!

"Ooh!" said Tuppeny, in fright. "I've
got the jug! Whatever shall I do with it? I
daren't take it back!"

"Where did you get it from?" asked his
mother, and he told her. She took it and
looked at it.

"Well, it's a pretty little jug," she said.
"If the gnome comes for it, he can have
it – but I'm not going to let you go back to
that cottage with it!"

"Let's use it," said Tuppeny, who
thought it was the prettiest jug he had ever
seen. "We'll keep the milk in it, Mother."

He poured the milk into it and put it on
the shelf. When teatime came, his mother
set it on the table with the other things.
Tuppeny looked to see what there was for
tea.

"Only dry bread!" he said in dismay.
"Oh, Mother, what a miserable tea – just
the same as breakfast and dinner."

"Well, times are very hard," said his mother with a sigh, pouring milk into the cups. "I wish I had cakes, butter and jam to give you, Tuppeny, but –"

She stopped in surprise – for on the table there suddenly appeared a dish of jam, a dish of yellow butter, and two plates of wonderful cakes!

"Ooh!" cried Tuppeny, in delight. "Look at that! Mother, that's a wishing jug, sure as eggs are eggs!"

He snatched it out of his mother's hand and wished again, pouring milk out as he did so, for he guessed that the little jug would not grant wishes unless something was poured out of it at the same time as the wish was wished.

"I wish for a cow of our own, a sheep and a pig!" cried the excited boy.

"Moo! Baa! Grunt!" came from behind him and there in the kitchen stood the three animals he had wished for! His mother cried out in astonishment and drove them into the yard.

"Be careful what you wish for, you silly boy," she said. "I don't want my little kitchen crowded out with farm animals."

"I wish for a big kitchen!" cried Tuppeny. "I wish for a big house! I wish for a garden, and a farm, and an orchard!"

In a twinkling the kitchen became a great, big, shining room with an enormous stove at one end. The cottage disappeared and a grand house arose in its place. The tiny garden became spacious grounds, and in the distance fields appeared dotted with sheep, horses and cows. A fine orchard came not far away, its trees laden with ripe fruit.

"My goodness!" shouted Tuppeny, in delight. "We're rich! We're grand! I can be a prince and marry a princess!"

The jug was empty by this time, so Tuppeny filled it with water and began pouring it out, wishing all the time.

"I wish for a suit of red and gold," he said, "and a feathered cap and flowing cloak. I want a glittering sword and a horse with nodding plumes. I want a hundred servants to follow me, each carrying a sack of gold or jewels. Ha, I'll be the grandest person in the land, and I'll go tomorrow and ask for the hand of Princess Melanie and marry her!"

As he wished, each wish came true. He was clad in red and gold, and a horse with nodding plumes appeared in the garden. A hundred servants walked up the broad path, each carrying a blue sack which Tuppeny guessed to be full of gold or jewels.

"Sleep in the garden," he commanded them, with a wave of his hand. "I shall not need you till tomorrow." The men obediently sank down on the grass and went to sleep. Tuppeny and his mother talked excitedly till his father came home, and stared in wonder at the great house that stood in the place of his cottage. Tuppeny ran out and dragged him indoors,

and the astonished man looked at the little red jug that had worked such wonders.

The next day Tuppeny set out to go to the palace of the King! He rode on his beautiful black horse, and a glittering sword hung by his side. His cloak of red and gold streamed out in the wind, and behind him walked his hundred servants with their sacks.

At midday he arrived at the palace gates and the sentries opened them to let in this magnificent youth with his great following.

"Tell His Majesty that Prince Tuppeny of Trim has come to see him," said the bold youth. The King, hearing how grand the youth looked, and what a number of servants he had, commanded him to be brought before him.

"Your Majesty, I have come to ask for your daughter's hand," said Tuppeny, bowing low.

The King laughed.

"I know nothing of you," he said. "Where do you come from?"

"From the great land of Trim," answered Tuppeny. " I have brought some presents for you, Sire."

His hundred servants came forward and emptied their sacks in front of the throne. The King stared in amazement. He had never seen so much gold, nor so many glittering jewels before. This must be a very rich prince, he thought!

The Princess Melanie was sitting beside her father. She was a pretty maiden, and she liked the look of Tuppeny. He was much nicer-looking than the old duke that her father had chosen for her to marry. She liked his merry, black eyes and curly hair.

"I'd like to marry this prince," she said. Tuppeny blushed with pleasure.

The King bade his daughter be silent.

"My daughter is already promised in marriage to the Duke of Waitabit," he said. "He has a castle ready for her, and a necklace of lovely diamonds."

"I will build her ten palaces, each lovelier than the other!" cried Tuppeny. "I will give her a hundred necklaces, a thousand brooches and as many dresses as she pleases to have!"

"Nonsense!" said the King. "No one is rich enough for that. If you could do as you say, I might give you my daughter, but such words are empty as air."

"Will you give me the Princess Melanie to be my wife if I build her ten palaces tonight?" asked Tuppeny, eagerly.

"Yes!" said the King, laughing. "I know quite well that such a thing can never be

done. But listen, boy – if you fail, I shall clap you in prison for a year! That will teach you to boast idly!"

Tuppeny bowed and went out. He took the little red jug from the leather bag in which he carried it, and filled it with water from a pump. Then he wished.

"I wish that ten palaces, each more beautiful than the last, may appear before the King's eyes tomorrow morning," he said. "And I wish that a hundred pages shall appear before the Princess Melanie carrying necklaces and brooches made of the most precious stones in the world, and that twenty maidens shall also appear, bringing with them dresses made of silks and satins, embroidered with silver and gold."

The next day Tuppeny went to the palace very early, and asked to be shown into the King's presence as soon as he was up. When the King at last received him, he bowed himself to the floor.

"Your Majesty," he said, "I come to claim the Princess Melanie. I would marry her today."

"Nonsense!" said the King, sharply.

"Don't be foolish. Where are these wonderful palaces you boasted of? Be off before I keep my word and clap you into prison."

"Your Majesty, pray come to the window," said Tuppeny. The King went to the window and leaned out. At that very moment the wonder happened. One by one ten gleaming palaces arose out of nothing, and stood around the King's own palace, glittering in their beauty, their towers and spires rising high in the sunlit air.

Then from each palace came ten pages carrying splendid necklaces and brooches on cushions of black velvet. Following them came the maidens with wonderful dresses for the delighted Princess Melanie who flung her arms round Tuppeny and kissed him.

"I shall marry you today!" she declared. "You are the most wonderful youth in the world! Oh, Father, think of having ten lovely palaces for my own, and all those jewels and dresses!"

"Well, I hope that your husband will kindly plant the palaces a little further off," said the King. "They are very

magnificent, but they spoil my view. Stop
hugging Prince Tuppeny, Melanie, and go
and get ready for your marriage. I suppose
I must keep my word and give you to the
prince."

What a to-do there was that day! The
princess was married to Tuppeny, and

all the people cheered madly when they saw the handsome pair driving through the streets in a carriage made of pure gold, drawn by twenty coal-black horses, each with a white star in the middle of its forehead. Tuppeny had wished for this, and the princess was simply delighted.

The next thing that Tuppeny did was to move the ten palaces a little further away, each on a hill which he had specially made for them. Then he and the Princess Melanie stayed a week in each one in turn, enjoying life very much indeed.

Tuppeny gave Melanie the wishing jug for a wedding present, and at first she used it every day, finding it great fun to have all her wishes come true, no matter what they were. Then she grew tired of it, and put it away in the china cupboard, forgetting all about it, for she had every single thing she wanted.

One day a beggar came to the kitchen door, and begged for a glass of water.

"Get it yourself from the pump in the yard," said the maid, rudely.

"Lend me a jug to get it with," said the man. The maid opened the door of the

china cupboard and looked for an old jug
to give him.

"That red one will do," said the man,
and the maid gave it to him. As soon as he
had it in his hands, he gave a loud laugh
and ran to the pump. It was the wizard!
He filled the jug with water and began to
wish. He wished the palaces to become
cottages, and all Tuppeny's lovely horses
to become mice. He wished and wished and
wished, and Tuppeny couldn't think what
was happening around him, for everything
began to change as the wizard wished.

At last Tuppeny rushed out to see what
was the matter – and there in the yard he
saw the wizard who had sent him into the

gnome's cottage to steal the red jug!

He saw the jug in the wizard's hand and rushed at him. He snatched at it, and the two began to wrestle for it. There was still a little water in it, and the wizard tried to pour it out and wish at the same time, but Tuppeny wouldn't let him.

"Give me the jug!" cried Tuppeny, hitting the wizard on the head.

"Ooh!" shouted the wizard in pain. "All right – you shall have the jug!"

He managed to pour out a little water and wished as he did so.

"I wish you away in a desert land!" he

cried. "And much good may the wishing jug do you there!"

In a trice Tuppeny had disappeared. He flew through the air and at last landed with a bump on yellow sand. All around him stretched a desolate country. Here and there were low bushes and stunted trees, but not a man or woman was to be seen.

"Well, never mind, I've got the wishing jug!" said Tuppeny. "I'll just wish myself home again and put everything right once more."

But alas, the jug was empty! It would not grant wishes unless something was poured out of it, and Tuppeny looked round for a stream or pond. But in that desolate country there was none.

All that day and the next poor Tuppeny wandered on and on looking for some water, but could find none.

"I shall die of thirst!" he groaned. "If it were not for these fruits that grow on the bushes, I should be dead already, the sun is so hot."

That night Tuppeny lay down to sleep in despair. He knew there was no water to be found – but in the night he awoke suddenly. Something soft and wet was falling on his face.

"It's raining!" cried Tuppeny, in joy. "It's raining! Where's my jug?"

He stood out in the rain – but the shower was soon over and there were very few drops in the jug.

Tuppeny poured them out and wished quickly before the jug was empty, wondering if the tiny amount of water was enough for a wish.

"I wish myself outside the pump at home!" he cried.

Yes! There was just enough water for a wish, for Tuppeny found himself flying through the air at a great pace and at last landed on his feet just beside the pump from which the wizard had filled the jug. Quickly Tuppeny filled it full, and wished loudly.

"Let everything be as it was two days ago!" he said – and hey presto, the palaces came back with a rush, the mice became horses, the princess came rushing down the steps, and Tuppeny shouted aloud in delight. Everything was as it was before.

"This jug is too dangerous to be left about," said Tuppeny, after he had hugged his Melanie. "If that wizard ever gets it again, we shall be in a bad way! Listen, darling Melanie – have you everything you want?"

"Everything!" said the princess.

"So have I!" said Tuppeny. "So I'll smash the jug and no one can ever wish us ill!"

He threw the little red jug on the ground and it smashed into a hundred pieces.

Each piece turned green, gave out a little spire of smoke and vanished.

"Ooh!" said Princess Melanie. "Did you see that?"

Tuppeny laughed. "I want a drink of lemonade," he said. "I'm dreadfully thirsty!"

"I'll get you some," said Melanie. "But Tuppeny, I'm sorry you broke the jug – it would have been such fun to show it to our children, and let them wish."

"We'll get the story of it written down for everyone to read!" said Tuppeny. "I'm sure they'll like it!"

And I hope you did!

Bushy's Secret

This is the story of a secret.

It was Bushy Squirrel's secret, and the secret was where he had hidden his nuts.

He had hidden them in the hollow oak-tree, and covered them with leaves. He thought it was such a clever place to think of.

"Nobody will ever look there," he said. "It's a secret, a secret, a secret! It's fun to have a secret! I won't tell anyone!"

"What won't you tell anyone?" asked Chitter-Chatter the magpie, who came flying by and heard Bushy talking to himself.

"I shan't tell anyone my secret!" said Bushy.

"Oh, do tell me," said Chitter-Chatter. "I won't tell anyone!" So Bushy told him. He whispered his secret in Chitter-

Chatter's little ear.

"This is my secret," he said, "I've hidden my nuts in the hollow oak-tree. Isn't it a clever place?"

"Very," said Chitter-Chatter, and flew off again.

Presently Chitter-Chatter spied Bobtail Bunny frisking down below, and he flew down to him.

"Good morning, Bobtail," he said. "I've just seen Bushy Squirrel. He's got a secret, and he told it to me."

"A secret! Oh, do tell me!" begged Bobtail. "I won't tell anyone!"

So Chitter-Chatter whispered the secret in Bobtail's soft ear.

"This is Bushy's secret," he said. "He's hidden his nuts in the hollow oak-tree. Isn't it a clever place?"

"Very!" said Bobtail, and scampered off.

He soon saw Prickles the hedgehog running along by a hedge, and he scampered up to him.

"Good morning, Prickles!" he said. "I've just seen Chitter-Chatter the magpie. He knows a secret, and he told it to me!"

"A secret! Oh, do tell me!" begged Prickles. "I won't tell anyone!"

So Bobtail Bunny whispered the secret in Prickles' spiky ear.

"This is the secret," he said. "Someone, I won't tell who, has hidden his nuts in the hollow oak-tree. Isn't it a clever place?"

"Very!" said Prickles, and ran off.

He soon met Frisky Squirrel, Bushy's cousin, and he hurried up to him.

"Good morning, Frisky," he said. "I've just seen Bobtail Bunny. He knows a secret and he told it to me."

"A secret! Oh, do tell me!" begged Frisky. "I won't tell anyone!"

So Prickles the hedgehog whispered the secret in Frisky's ear.

"This is the secret," he said. "Someone has hidden his nuts in the hollow oak-tree. Isn't it a clever place?"

"Very!" said Frisky, and leaped away to the hollow oak-tree.

On his way he met Bushy Squirrel.

"Good morning, Bushy," he said. "I've just seen Prickles the hedgehog. He knows a secret, and he told it to me."

"A secret! How lovely! I've got a secret too!" said Bushy. "Do tell me the secret you know! I won't tell anyone!"

So Frisky whispered the secret in Bushy's sharp ear.

"This is the secret," he said. "Someone has hidden his nuts in the hollow oak-tree! Isn't it a clever place? Come along and find them, Bushy! We'll have a lovely feast!"

"But that's my secret!" wailed Bushy. "It's my secret! They're my nuts! I thought no one would think of such a clever place!"

"Oh, everybody knows!" said Frisky in surprise. "Prickles told me. I forget who told Prickles."

"I'm going to ask him," said Bushy crossly, and off he went.

"Who told you my secret, Prickles?" he asked when he found him.

"Bobtail Bunny did," said Prickles, "but I forget who told him."

Bushy went to find Bobtail Bunny.

"Who told you my secret, Bobtail?" he asked, when he found him.

"Chitter-Chatter the magpie did!" said Bobtail. "He said you told him your secret, Bushy!"

"So I did, so I did!" said Bushy. "And I wish I hadn't. Oh dear, dear me! I suppose I must go and hide my nuts somewhere else now!"

But when he looked for them, they were gone! That rascally squirrel Frisky had taken them.

"And all because nobody could keep a secret!" wept poor Bushy. "Well, I'll remember next time that the only way to keep a secret is to keep it yourself!"

The Wrong
Lunch-Time

"Mummy, may we go and play in the fields at the bottom of the garden today?" asked Ann. "It's such a lovely day, and we won't sit down on the damp grass. The little lambs are in the field, and it's fun to watch them."

"Very well," said her mother, "but you must come when I call you. I shall come to the kitchen door and call 'Cuckoo!' loudly – and you must cuckoo back and come straight in to lunch."

"Yes, we promise to do that," said Gerry. "We won't be a minute late!"

Off they went. Gerry took his box of toy soldiers, and Ann took her favourite doll.

"I can put my toy soldiers out on the top of one of the hen-houses in the field," said Gerry. "They will look fine, all shining in the sun."

"And I shall take my doll for a walk all round the field and back," said Ann. "I might find one or two primroses by the stream. If I do, Dolly can wear them in her hair."

Gerry put out all his soldiers one by one and marched them up the hen-house. They did look grand. Ann took her doll round the field and found four primroses. She was so pleased. She put two in her own hair and two in Dolly's.

"Come and see my soldiers, Ann!"

shouted Gerry. "They are all in a long line!"

Ann ran over to look at them – and just then a sound came to their ears.

"Cuckoo!"

"Goodness! It's lunch-time already!" said Ann, in dismay. "And we've hardly been here any time. Hurry up and put your soldiers away, Gerry. You know what Mummy said – we were to come at once."

"All right," said Gerry, and he scooped all his soldiers into the box. He put the lid on and the two children trotted back home. They went indoors and found their mother washing some cups at the sink.

"What are you back here for?" she asked in surprise. "I thought you went to play in the field."

"Well, you called us in," said Ann. "We came at once."

"Bless us, child, I didn't call you!" said her mother. "It's only twelve o'clock. You've another hour till lunch-time."

"But, Mum, we heard you call us," said Gerry.

"Well, you heard wrong then," said their mother, wiping the cups dry. " Go

along now. I expect it was someone else you heard."

Ann and Gerry ran off again. This time Gerry took his wooden train and Ann took her ball. Soon they were back in the field with the lambs again, and Ann was throwing her ball up and catching it. The lambs came round to watch, and when she missed the ball, so that it went bouncing towards them on the grass, they skipped off on their funny little legs, pretending to be quite frightened.

Gerry filled his wooden engine with stones and pretended that he was taking goods from place to place. Just as he was filling it for the third time, he stood up and listened.

"Ann!" he cried. "Time to go home, I heard Mum calling."

"You didn't!" said Ann.

"I did!" said Gerry.

"Didn't!" said Ann.

"Well, listen then, and see," said Gerry. So they listened – and sure enough, Ann heard "Cuckoo!"

"Sorry, Gerry," she said. "You're right. It is Mummy – but I didn't think it could possibly be one o'clock."

Back home they went at top speed – and this time their mother was hanging out some clothes in the garden.

"Back again!" she said in astonishment. "What's brought you home again so soon?"

"But you called us again!" said Ann, in the greatest surprise. "You did really. We both heard you."

"Darling, I didn't call you," said their mother. "It's not quite half-past twelve."

"Well, who could it be, then, calling us like that?" said Gerry, puzzled.

"Let's go back to the fields and see if we can see anyone hiding," said Ann. "Oh,

Gerry – it might be a fairy! Just playing us a trick, you know!"

They ran back to the field and hunted carefully all round the hedge. Then they heard the voice again, "Cuckoo!"

"There *is* some one hiding near by," said Ann. "I heard that call again – and I'm sure it's not Mummy this time. Oh, do let's find whoever it is, Gerry."

But although they hunted everywhere, not a boy or a girl or a pixie could they see. Not one. It was most disappointing.

"Cuckoo! Cuckoo!" The children heard a voice in the distance and saw their mother waving to them.

"It is Mummy this time!" said Ann. "Come on, Gerry."

They ran home for the third time – and it was their mother calling them. As they washed their hands they told her how puzzled they were. As they were telling her, a voice called clearly, not far off, "Cuckoo!"

"Did you hear that?" said Ann excitedly. "Do you suppose it's a fairy having a joke?"

Their mother laughed till the tears ran down her face. "My dears," she said, "what silly-billies you are! That's the cuckoo, come back again for the summer! He's been calling all morning! Did you really think it was me who was calling so often?"

"The cuckoo!" cried the children in

delight, and rushed to the door at once. Sure enough, it was – they heard his clear call coming down the hillside, "Cuckoo! Cuckoo!"

"Cuckoo!" the children shouted back. "You tricked us this morning, cuckoo, and made us go home twice for nothing, but we're very glad you're back again!"

"Cuckoo!" shouted the cuckoo – and they heard him all the time they were having lunch. He was just as glad to be back as they were glad to have him!

The
Goblin's Dog

Once upon a time there lived a little boy called Willie. He had a dog named Tinker, and they often went for walks together.

Tinker was fond of Willie, but the little boy was not very kind to his dog. He was supposed to look after him and care for him, but many a time he went off to play and forgot all about him.

Tinker lived in a kennel out in the yard. It was a nice kennel, but it needed new straw each day. Sometimes Willie remembered, and sometimes he didn't.

Tinker liked fresh water to drink, but often Willie forgot all about refilling his water bowl. And once poor Tinker had no water at all because someone had upset it, and Willie hadn't noticed.

"Willie, it's cold weather now," his mother said to him one day. "Have you

44

seen that Tinker has plenty of good warm straw in his kennel?"

"Yes, Mother," said Willie. But, you know, he hadn't – and Tinker had made his old straw so flat that there was no warmth in it at all. So he was cold at night when the frosts came. He thought of Willie in his warm bed, and how he longed to be able to curl up there with him. But he had to stay in his icy-cold kennel.

Now one night a small brownie came by on the way to the dairy to get a drink of milk. He heard Tinker shivering and popped his head into the kennel.

"What's the matter with you?" he said.

"You seem very cold! Haven't you any warm straw?"

"Not much," said Tinker. "And my water is frozen too, so that I can't get a drink if I want to. Willie didn't take me for a run, either, so I haven't been able to get warm. Do you think you could bring me some water, brownie? There is some in the stream not far away."

"Certainly," said the brownie. He broke the ice in the bowl, emptied it out, and ran to the stream. He came back with some water and put it beside the kennel. "I wish I could get you some straw, too," he said. "But I don't know where there is any."

"Never mind," said Tinker gratefully. "Perhaps Willie will remember to get some tomorrow."

The brownie went to the dairy and had a drink of milk. He was unhappy because he couldn't forget the poor cold dog. He wished he could get some straw. He remembered that a wizard lived not far off, and he thought that maybe he would know how to make straw out of magic. So he went to his house and knocked.

A black cat opened the door and the

brownie went in. Soon he had told the wizard all about Tinker. The wizard listened, and he frowned deeply.

"That boy should be taught a lesson," he said. He clapped his hands, and the black cat appeared.

"Fetch the policeman," said the wizard. The cat disappeared, and when it came back, it brought with it a large policeman with pink wings and a shiny face.

"Go and arrest Willie, who lives at the Farm House," commanded the wizard. "Bring him before the court tomorrow, charged with neglecting his dog."

The policeman saluted, flapped his pink wings and disappeared.

And soon, what a shock poor Willie got! He was sound asleep when he awoke to find a lantern shining on his face. The shiny-faced policeman was standing near by, and he spoke sternly to Willie.

"Come with me, little boy. I arrest you for neglecting your dog!"

Willie put on his coat and went with the policeman. The big policeman suddenly spread his wings and flew through the night, carrying Willie firmly

in his arms. There was no escape at all!

The little boy spent the night at the wizard's, and then the next morning the policeman took him to a big courthouse. Inside there was a judge who sat solemnly at a high bench, and had great wings like a butterfly's wings behind him. There were twelve pixies, brownies, and gnomes sitting at a table below, and there were six policemen, all with pink wings.

"This is Willie," said the policeman who had fetched the little boy. "He is here because of the following things: forgetting to give his dog fresh water – forgetting to give him straw for his kennel – forgetting to take him for a run – and altogether being very unkind."

"Very bad," said the judge, frowning at Willie. "Very bad indeed! Jurymen, what punishment shall we have?"

The twelve pixies, brownies, and gnomes who sat below the judge began to talk excitedly among themselves. Then a long-bearded gnome stood up.

"If you please, your worship," he said to the judge. "We think he should be turned into a dog and sent to one of the goblins."

"Certainly, certainly," said the judge. "A very good idea!"

"But you can't do that!" cried poor Willie. "Why, my mother would wonder where I am!"

"Well, we will make your dog Tinker change into you," said the judge. "It will be a treat for him to have good food, plenty of fresh water to drink, and a warm bed at night. Now stand still, please, Willie!"

Willie stood still, wondering what was going to happen. The judge took up a wand that lay beside him, leaned over to Willie, and tapped him on the shoulder, saying, "A curious punishment you'll see! A boy you are – a dog you'll be!"

And then he said a very magic word – and my goodness me, Willie found that black hair was growing all over his body! His clothes disappeared. He grew a long tail. His ears became furry. His nose became long – he had paws instead of his hands and feet. He was a little black dog, and when he opened his

mouth to speak, he could only say "Woof, woof, woof!"

"Take him to the goblin Workalot,"

commanded the judge. So Willie was led out of the court on a chain, and taken to a small cottage in a wood. Here a little green goblin lived. He didn't seem at all pleased to see Willie.

"I don't really want a dog," he said to the policeman who brought Willie. "Dogs are a nuisance. But if the judge says I'm to have him, I suppose I must."

51

There was no kennel for Willie so he hoped he would sleep on a nice warm rug in front of the kitchen fire. But a big grey cat suddenly appeared as soon as Willie sat down on the rug.

"Phizzz-ss-ss-ss!" she hissed at poor Willie. He ran back in fright, and got between the legs of the goblin who was just coming in with a bowl of water. Down went the goblin, and all the water splashed over Willie.

"Clumsy creature!" cried Workalot. He gave Willie a cuff on the head. Willie hoped he would get a towel and dry him, but he didn't. So the dog sat in a corner and shivered, for he did not dare to go near the fire when the cat was there.

Workalot was a very busy goblin. He ran here and there, he did this and that, and he grumbled and talked to himself all the time. The grey cat did nothing, but when Workalot needed help with a spell, she walked up and sat solemnly in the middle of a big chalk circle.

Soon Willie began to feel very hungry indeed. The cat had a good dinner of fish and milk put down for her, but the goblin did not give Willie any dinner.

"I'll give you something later on!" he grumbled. But he quite forgot, so poor Willie had to go without. He thought he would whine so that Workalot would take notice of him. But as soon as he began yelping and whining, the goblin lost his temper. Willie put his tail down and ran under the table. But the goblin pulled him out, took him to the door, and put him outside.

It was pouring with rain. Willie looked round for shelter, but there was only one bush growing in the garden. He ran to that and crouched underneath, cold, wet

and hungry. How dreadful it was to be a dog owned by an unkind master with no love in him!

The rain stopped. Willie crept out from the bush, but the door was shut and he could not get into the house. He looked at the house next door. A dog lived there too. But it was a dog that somebody loved, for it was well-brushed, cheerful, and not at all thin. Willie wished he belonged to a good home too. How lovely it would be to be petted and well looked after!

The door opened and the goblin whistled. Willie ran in. The cat spat at him and Willie growled back. Workalot gave him a cuff. "Leave my cat alone!" he said. "Go into the corner and lie down."

Willie lay down. The cat sat in front of the warm fire and washed herself. There was an empty bowl not far from her, and Willie felt sure that it had been put down for him – with some meat and biscuits in, perhaps – and the cat had eaten it all up.

Willie fell asleep at last. But when night came, the goblin woke him up by fastening a chain to his collar and dragging him outside. He had put an old barrel there, on its side, and in the barrel he had put a handful of straw. "Get in!" said the goblin. "And mind you bark if the enemy comes!"

Poor Willie! He didn't know who the enemy was – and he was very frightened to think they might come! He was cold too, for the wind blew right into his barrel, and he was so thirsty that he would have been glad to lick the snow, if there had been any. He began to whine dismally.

Out flew the goblin in a fine rage, and shouted at him.

After that, Willie didn't dare to make

another sound. He just lay silent and hoped that the enemy wouldn't come.

Suddenly, at midnight, he heard a little scraping sound at the gate and he stiffened in fear. The enemy! The gate swung open – and in came, whoever do you think? Why, nobody else but Tinker the dog! He ran up to Willie's barrel and sniffed at him.

"I heard you were here, changed into a dog," he said. "They changed me into you – but I changed back at midnight and I've come to rescue you. You were never very kind to me, Willie, but I love you, and

would do anything for you. Now keep still and I'll gnaw right through your collar."

Willie was full of gratitude to the little dog. He kept still, and very soon Tinker's sharp teeth had bitten right through the leather. He was free!

"Come on!" whispered Tinker. "I know the way."

The two dogs sped through the night, and at last came to the Farm House. "Go to your room and get into your bed," said Tinker. "In the morning you will be yourself."

Willie pushed his way into the house and ran up the stairs. He jumped into his warm bed and was soon asleep. In the morning he was himself again.

"It's all very strange," thought Willie, as he dressed. "How kind Tinker was! How awful it is to be a dog belonging to an unkind master. I have been unkind to Tinker often. I never will be again!"

He ran down into the yard. Tinker was in his kennel. He wagged his tail. "Tinker! Tinker!" said Willie, putting his arms round the little dog. "Thank you for rescuing me! I'm sorry I was unkind to you. I will always love you now, and look after you properly!"

And so he did. Tinker has a warm kennel, plenty of fresh water each day, good food, a fine walk in the morning, and lots of pats. He is very happy – and I do hope your dog is, too!

Mary Brown and
Mary Contrary

Mary was out for a walk. She took with her Josephine, her biggest doll, and wheeled her in her pram. It was a lovely day, and the sun shone brightly.

Mary went a long way. She walked down the little green path in Bluebell Wood to get out of the hot sun – but dear me, when she turned back, she found that she had lost her way!

Somehow or other she must have taken the wrong path – and now she didn't know how to get back. She was most upset.

"Never mind," she said to herself. "I shall soon meet someone, and then I can ask them the way to my home."

In a few minutes she did meet someone. It was a little fat man in a red tunic. He was hurrying along with a hen under his arm. Mary called to him.

"Please," she said, "I've lost my way. Can you tell me how to get home?"

"What is your name?" asked the fat man.

"I'm Mary," said the little girl, "and this is Josephine, one of my dolls."

"How do you do, Mary, how do you do, Josephine," said the little man, raising his pointed cap politely. "Yes, certainly I can show you your way home. Come with me."

Mary followed him through the wood, pushing Josephine before her in her pram. She walked down the narrow green path – and at last, to her great surprise, she came out into a little village.

What a strange village! The cottages were very tiny indeed, and at the doors and in the gardens stood children dressed in strange suits and frocks. They looked just as if they had come out of her nursery rhyme book.

"Why, those two might be Jack and Jill!" thought Mary, looking at a boy and girl who stood holding a pail between them. "And that boy singing all by himself there is just like Tommy Tucker. Look at that girl sitting on a stool too – she's just like

Miss Muffet eating her curds and whey!"

"We're nearly there," said the little man.

"I don't seem to know this way home," Mary said.

"Don't you?" asked the fat man in surprise, and his hen clucked loudly under his arm, as if she too was surprised. "Well – here you are. There's your cottage, look!"

Mary looked. They had stopped just outside a trim little cottage whose walls were painted white. At the windows hung bright curtains, and the door was painted yellow. It was a dear little cottage.

"But that isn't my home!" said Mary. "You've made a mistake!"

"Well, didn't you say that you were Mary?" the little man asked her in astonishment. "This is Mary's cottage. Look, there's the name on the gate."

Mary looked. Sure enough, on the gate the words "Mary's Cottage" were painted.

"And look – there are your cockleshells making a nice border to your flower-

62

beds," said the little man, pointing. "And there are your pretty Canterbury bells, all flowering nicely in the sunshine."

Mary stared at the cottage garden. She saw that each flowerbed was neatly edged with cockleshells, and that wonderful Canterbury bells flowered everywhere, their blossoms just like silver bells, instead of being blue or white.

"And there are your pretty maids all in a row!" said the little man, waving his hand to where a row of pretty dolls sat on the grass. "Look, your doll wants to join them."

To Mary's great astonishment she saw her doll Josephine getting out of the pram! Josephine walked through the garden gate and sat herself down in the row of dolls, who seemed very pleased to see her. Then the wind blew and all the Canterbury Bells began to ring – tinkle-tinkle-tinkle!

Mary was too surprised to speak. She couldn't understand it at all – and yet she felt she had seen all this before somewhere. Was it in a book?

"Isn't this your home?" asked the little man, looking puzzled. "Your name is Mary

Quite Contrary, isn't it?"

"No, it isn't!" cried Mary, seeing how he had made his mistake. "I'm just Mary Brown! You thought I was some other Mary – the Mary of the nursery rhyme. You know: Mary, Mary, quite contrary, how does your garden grow? With silver bells and cockleshells, and pretty maids all in a row."

"Well, of course I thought you were!" said the little man. "I'm so sorry. I've brought you ever so far out of your way."

Just then the door of the cottage opened and a little girl about Mary's age came out. She was a pretty little girl with long curly hair, and she had a big sun-bonnet on her head. Her dress reached right to her shoes, and her little feet twinkled in and out as she walked.

"I say, Mary Quite Contrary!" called the little man. "I've made a dreadful mistake. This little girl's name is Mary, and I've brought her to your cottage thinking she lived here – and she doesn't!"

"Dear me!" said Mary Contrary, in a soft little voice. "What a pity! But never mind – she had better come in and rest for a little

while and then she shall have lunch with me. I'll see that she gets home all right."

Mary was delighted. She liked Mary Contrary very much indeed. It would be lovely to have lunch with her. She said goodbye to the little man who had made the mistake, and he hurried off down the street with the hen under his arm clucking loudly.

Mary walked into the garden, and the

other Mary took her into her spick-and-span cottage. It was so pretty inside, very small, like a doll's-house, but quite big enough for the two children.

"It's so hot that I thought of having ice-cream pudding and ginger beer for lunch today," said Mary Contrary. "I hope that will suit you all right, Mary."

"Oh yes!" said Mary, delighted. "I think that's just about the nicest lunch I ever heard of!"

Mary Contrary bustled about getting the table laid and Mary Brown helped her. Then they sat down to the largest ice-cream pudding Mary had ever seen – and do you know, they finished it between them! Then they had a bottle of ginger beer each. It was really lovely.

"This is the village of Nursery Rhyme," said Mary Contrary. "Tom the Piper's Son lives over there – he's a very naughty boy, always being beaten for stealing pigs. I don't have much to do with him! Next door lives Jack Horner, but he has a very good opinion of himself – he's always saying that he is a good boy!"

"Yes, I know all about him," said Mary

Brown. "Does Humpty-Dumpty live here too?"

"Yes," said Mary Contrary. "But, you know, he's very silly. He's been warned heaps of times not to sit on walls – but he always will. Then he falls off, and as he is a great big egg, he breaks, and there's such a mess to clear up. All the King's horses and all the King's men can't mend him. But he's all right again by the morning – and off he goes to sit on the wall once more!"

"I wish I could see him," said Mary, excited. "This is a lovely place, I think. Does Polly Flinders live here too?"

"Yes, but she's a dirty little girl," said

Mary Contrary, wrinkling up her nose in disgust. "She sits among the cinders and spoils all her nice new clothes. So her mother has to whip her. There is the Black Sheep here too. He doesn't belong to Bo-Peep, though – all her sheep are white. She's a silly girl, she's always losing them."

"But they come home all right, don't they?" asked Mary anxiously.

"Oh yes, and they always bring their tails behind them," answered Mary Contrary. "Will you have some more ginger beer? No? Well, now what about getting you home? I'll walk part of the way with you, and perhaps you wouldn't mind giving one of my pretty maids – my dolls, you know – a ride in Josephine's pram for a treat?"

"Of course!" said Mary, smiling. She went to the pram and made room beside Josephine. "I know Josephine would love to have someone in the pram with her."

So Mary Contrary tucked Esmeralda, her best pretty maid, into the pram beside Josephine, and the two dolls were very happy to be with one another. Mary loved to see her own doll smiling so cheerfully.

Off the two little girls went. Mary looked excitedly at all the little houses she passed. A little girl with a red cloak and hood stood at the door of one and Mary felt sure she was Red Riding Hood. She saw Johnny Thin who put the cat in the well, and Johnny Stout, who pulled him out. She waved to the Old Woman who lived in

a shoe, and wished she could go nearer to
the funny old house in the shape of a shoe
and look at it. But she was afraid that the
Old Woman might think she was one of
her many children, and whip her and put
her to bed.

At last they left the strange little village
behind and went into the wood. It wasn't
very long before they were on the right
path to Mary's home.

"Well, you know the way now," said
Mary Contrary, kissing Mary Brown. "Do
come and see me again, won't you? And be
sure to bring Josephine with you to visit
my pretty maids."

She took Esmeralda out of the pram,
kissed Josephine goodbye, and stood
waving to Mary as she went along the
green path. Mary hurried along, anxious
to tell her mother all her adventures.

Mary's mother was surprised! She
couldn't believe her ears!

"Well, you come with me, Mummy, next
time I go to see Mary Contrary," promised
Mary Brown. "I know you'll love to see
everybody!"

So her mother is going with her

tomorrow. I do hope they find the right path, don't you?

Treacle-Pudding
Town

Thomas loved treacle pudding. His mother used to make great big ones for her four children, with golden syrup poured all over them. Thomas thought it was the nicest pudding in the world.

He was greedy. He ate up his slice of pudding as quickly as he could, so that he could have a second helping before anyone else did.

"Don't gobble, Thomas," his mother said. But he gobbled because he wanted to have more than anybody else, so he went on gobbling.

He gobbled his bread-and-butter at tea-time so that he could have more cakes than anybody, especially if there was a chocolate cake. The other children were cross with him. "It isn't fair," they said. "You are greedy, Thomas, and you always try to have more than your fair share!"

One day there was a fine treacle pudding for lunch. Thomas had two big helpings – and then his mother said the rest of the pudding was to be saved for Ellen, his sister, who was going to be late for lunch that day. Thomas watched his mother put it into the larder. He longed and longed for just one more piece, although he had really had quite enough.

His mother went out into the garden to put some clothes on the line. Thomas opened the larder door and peeped inside.

There was the rest of the treacle pudding, still on the dish, warm and sticky! Thomas looked and looked at it.

And then, what do you think he did? He took a spoon and gobbled up the rest of that pudding!

Wasn't he horrid! When he had finished it all, he was frightened. What would his mother say? What would his sister do? She would smack him hard and pull his hair, because when she flew into a temper, she was very rough.

Thomas ran down the garden, squeezed through the hedge at the bottom, and sat in the field there.

"I do wish I needn't go home again," he said to himself. "I shall get into trouble when I do!" He sighed a heavy sigh, and a small man hurrying by stopped and looked at him in surprise.

"What's the matter?" he asked.

"Oh, I just don't want to go back home," said Thomas. "I know I shall be told off if I do."

"Poor boy!" said the man. He had a long beard reaching nearly to his toes, and the brightest green eyes that Thomas had ever seen. "Well, why go home? Isn't there somewhere else you can go?"

"No," said Thomas. "But oh, how I wish I could go to some place where I could have treacle pudding and chocolate cake, as much as ever I liked! I never have enough at home."

"Dear, dear!" said the little man. He was a brownie, though Thomas didn't know this. "Well, I think I can help you. What about coming with me to Treacle-Pudding Town? It's not very far."

Thomas could hardly believe his ears. Treacle-Pudding Town! What a wonderful place it sounded. He jumped up at once.

"I'll go," he said. "Is there really plenty of treacle pudding there?"

"Oh yes," said the brownie. "And chocolate cake too. It's a famous place for that, you know. They do nothing there but make and sell treacle puddings and chocolate cake. My cousin lives there. I'll take you to stay with him if you like. He'll be pleased to have you."

Well, greedy little Thomas was only too pleased to go. He forgot that his mother would worry about him. He forgot that he had promised to tidy his bedroom after lunch. He just wanted to get to those puddings and cakes. So off he went with the brownie.

He went across the field, over the stile, and into the wood. And in the very middle of the wood was Treacle-Pudding Town! Thomas stood and stared at it. It was a most extraordinary place.

"Why, the houses are the shape of treacle puddings and cakes!" he said. "How funny! And look at that stream – I'm sure it's full of treacle instead of water!"

"Here is my cousin's house," said the brownie, going into a tiny house shaped

Treacle-Pudding Town

77

like a birthday cake. The chimneys looked like three candles smoking!

"Tippy, Tippy, are you in?" cried the brownie. "I've brought a friend to stay with you."

"Very pleased to have him, I'm sure," said Tippy, who was a little man very like his cousin. He smelled of chocolate. In fact, the whole village smelled of chocolate and treacle. Thomas liked it.

"Well, goodbye, Thomas," said the first brownie. "I hope you'll have a good time. You can eat as much as ever you like here, you know."

Thomas was so excited. "Can I really?" he said. "I didn't have much lunch. Can I have some treacle pudding?"

"Certainly," said Tippy. He went to the kitchen and came back with a white dish in which was a steaming hot pudding with yellow treacle poured all over it. "Help yourself. I don't want any."

Well, you may not believe it, but Thomas ate all that treacle pudding!

Tippy saw the empty dish and grinned. "I've another pudding in the kitchen," he said. "Will you have it?"

But, dear me, Thomas felt as if he couldn't eat even a small slice. He shook his head. "I feel as if I want to go to sleep," he said.

"I should think so," said Tippy. He showed Thomas a couch, and the little boy lay down on it. He slept till teatime. Then he woke up. He smelled chocolate cakes baking and was glad.

"Hello!" said Tippy, coming in to lay the tea-table. "Teatime! New cakes!"

Thomas got up and sat at the table. Tippy put three plates on the table – one had small chocolate buns on it, one had a round chocolate cake, and one had a square one.

"Ha! No bread-and-butter!" said Thomas, pleased.

"Oh no," said Tippy. "Just cakes. Help yourself. I don't want any."

Thomas thought it was funny not to want any. Anyway, that left all the more for him! He ate all the little buns. He ate half the round chocolate cake, and then he began on the square one – but, oh dear, what a pity, before he was halfway through it, he suddenly felt as if he didn't want any more! What a waste of a cake! He drank his tea and went outside.

All the shops sold treacle puddings

and chocolate cakes. Nothing else at all! Thomas looked into two or three windows and then he got rather bored with seeing the same things, and wished he could find a toyshop. But there wasn't one.

He found some brownie children and played with them for a long time. They liked him, and asked him to go back to their home to have supper with them.

Thomas was feeling hungry again. It was a long time since teatime. He went to their house, wondering what there would be for supper.

What do you suppose it was? Yes – a great big treacle pudding! Thomas stared at it. He wasn't so pleased to see it as he had been to see the one at lunch-time. But all the same, he managed to eat two helpings of it. Then he went back to Tippy's house and undressed to go to bed.

In the morning he was very hungry again. He wondered if there would be bacon or kippers or eggs for breakfast, and perhaps corn flakes or porridge, and toast and marmalade. Lovely! He ran downstairs.

But, good gracious, Tippy brought in a

treacle pudding for breakfast! Thomas was really disappointed.

"You don't look pleased to see my beautiful pudding," said Tippy, offended. "Well, there's nothing else. I haven't baked any chocolate cakes yet. Eat up your pudding."

So Thomas ate it up, but somehow he didn't enjoy it. He was getting very tired of treacle pudding. And he was even more tired of it when lunch-time came and he found that there was nothing but chocolate buns and treacle pudding again. He felt as if he really couldn't eat any!

"If only it was rice pudding or stewed apples!" said Thomas to Tippy. Tippy looked as cross as could be.

"You horrid, ungrateful boy!" he said. "What did you want to come to Treacle-Pudding Town for? My cousin said you were a very greedy boy and would love to eat as much treacle pudding and chocolate cake as I could cook for you – and now, the very first lunch-time you are here, you turn up your nose at my nice pudding. Eat it up at once, I tell you!"

"I can't!" said poor Thomas. "I should

be ill if I did. It looks horrid to me now, somehow, that treacle pudding!"

Tippy was very angry. He picked up the treacle pudding and threw it straight at Thomas. It hit him on the nose and the treacle ran down his face. Then Tippy snowballed him with the chocolate buns. Thomas ran out of the house, crying. He was very unhappy and wanted his mother.

He ran through the town. He ran through the wood. He climbed over the stile and ran across the field back to his

home. He rushed up the garden and into the kitchen. There was his mother, baking chocolate cakes.

"Mother! Mother!" cried Thomas, hugging her. "Did you wonder where I had been all this time?"

"No, Thomas," said his mother in surprise. "It is only an hour since lunch."

Then Thomas knew that a day in Treacle-Pudding Town was only an hour in our world, and he was glad. But there was something he had to tell his mother.

"Mother," he said, "please forgive me – but I ate the rest of the treacle pudding out of the larder."

"Oh, Thomas, how naughty of you!" said his mother, shocked. "It's a good thing that Ellen has stayed to lunch at school after all. You must never do such a thing again – but I will forgive you, because you have told me. Thomas, don't be a greedy little boy – no one likes greedy children."

"I won't be greedy any more," promised Thomas.

"I expect you will be, though, at tea-time, when you see new chocolate buns on the table!" said his mother. But she got a surprise, for Thomas wouldn't eat a single chocolate bun! And he won't eat treacle pudding either! He can't bear to see one on the table. His mother doesn't know why, so she can't understand it – but I know why Thomas has changed, don't you?

Heyho and the
North Wind

Once upon a time Heyho the brownie was washing his clothes on a very windy day. He washed a pair of blue socks, six blue handkerchiefs, a red shirt and a yellow tunic. Then he took up his lovely new scarf and put that into the soapy water too.

Heyho was very proud of his scarf. It was yellow with an orange border, and was the nicest one in the whole of his village. The Fairy Queen herself had given it to him for a present when he had once stopped her runaway rabbits. They were pulling her carriage, and had been frightened at something – and off they went through the woods, helter-skelter, with the frightened Fairy Queen pulling hard at the reins.

Then Heyho had run out from the bushes and caught hold of the reins, stopping the rabbits at once. The Queen was very grateful, and by the next post had come the lovely yellow scarf in return for the brownie's bravery.

So you can guess Heyho was proud of it, and he washed it very carefully indeed. Then he wrung it out and hung it up on the line to dry. Eight-Legs the spider had given him some of his strongest thread and it made a very nice washing-line.

Heyho emptied his washtub and put the soap away. Then he went indoors to make himself a cup of cocoa, for he was rather thirsty after so much washing.

"It's a good thing it's such a windy day," said Heyho to himself. "It will dry the clothes quickly."

"Whoo-oo-oo!" roared the wind outside. It was the North Wind, and it sounded excited. It flapped the clothes to and fro and they all danced up and down.

Heyho finished his cocoa and went outside to see if his clothes were drying. He felt the socks – yes, nearly dry. He felt the handkerchiefs – yes, quite dry – and the tunic and shirt were hardly wet at all – and the scarf – but dear me, where was the scarf?

Heyho's heart almost stopped beating. He looked up and down the line but there was no scarf to be seen. It was gone! What a dreadful thing!

The pegs were still there. The North Wind must have torn the scarf away and taken it for himself!

"He saw it and thought it would do nicely for him, I expect," thought Heyho. "Oh, my lovely, lovely scarf that the Fairy Queen gave me! I must get it back, I really must!"

He sat down on the grass and wondered

how he could get it back. He scratched his chin hard, rubbed his nose, and frowned deeply. Then he thought of an idea.

"I'll go to the North Wind's house and ask him what he has done with it!" he said, jumping to his feet. "He has no right to steal my scarf like that! I'll make him give it back to me!"

So he locked up his little house, and took the key to Twiddle, his next-door neighbour.

"Where are you going all of a sudden?" asked Twiddle in surprise.

"To the house of the North Wind," said Heyho, fiercely. "He has stolen my scarf, and I'm going to get it back!"

"Oh, Heyho, you are brave!" cried Twiddle. "The North Wind is very big and very strong. I should be afraid to go and see him. People say that he has a dreadful temper too!"

"Well, I hope I come back all right," said Heyho, feeling a bit shaky. "Anyway, here's my key, Twiddle. Keep it for me, will you?"

So Twiddle said he would, and Heyho marched off northwards. He went up seven hills and down again. He crossed ten rivers, and went over twelve stiles. He walked through five woods, and then far away in the distance he saw the mountain on the top of which was the house of the North Wind.

It was very cold. Snowflakes floated about in the air and Heyho wished that he had his nice warm scarf tied tightly round his neck. He felt very cross indeed with the North Wind. He began to climb the mountain, and soon he was quite out of breath. He would never have got to the top if a large eagle had not kindly offered him a lift.

"My nest is nearly at the top," said the eagle. "I will take you as far as that, if you like."

So Heyho gladly climbed on to the bird's soft back, and soon he was nearly at the top of the steep mountain. The eagle shook him off, and he said thank you, and went on again up the winding path.

Soon he saw the house of the North Wind. It was a funny sort of house, for,

although it had openings for windows and doors, it had no glass in the windows and no doors in the entrances. Heyho thought it must be a very cold house to live in.

At last he got to the front doorway. He could see no sign of the North Wind, but he heard a loud snoring noise. He peeped in at the front doorway, and at first saw nothing. Then he made out a great bed, and lying on it was the North Wind, an enormous person, very billowy looking. He was fast asleep and snoring.

"Oh dear!" thought Heyho. "He won't be very pleased at being wakened up."

The brownie stood and looked at the North Wind for a few minutes, and then he made up his mind. He must wake him! So he stepped into the doorway and went up to the bed.

"Hey, North Wind!" he said. "Wake up!"

The North Wind didn't stir. So Heyho shouted more loudly still:

"Hey, North Wind! Wake up, I say!"

He poked the North Wind with his finger and made him stir. Then with an enormous yawn the wind sat up and rubbed his eyes. He looked so big that

Heyho's knees began to shake and he could hardly stand up.

Then the North Wind suddenly saw Heyho, and stared in surprise.

"What did you wake me for?" he asked crossly.

"I've come to ask you to give me back my yellow scarf," Heyho said boldly. "You took it this morning."

"What? You've come to wake me up for a silly thing like that!" cried the North Wind, angrily. "I'll blow you to the other end of the world!"

He stooped down and was just going to blow the brownie right out of the house when Heyho caught hold of his nose and held on tight. That just saved him, for though he was lifted right off his feet by the force of the wind, he wasn't blown away.

"Ow! Oh!" cried the North Wind. "Let go of my nose, you horrid little brownie!"

"Well, don't blow me away, then!" said Heyho. "And let me tell you this, North Wind – the Fairy Queen will be very angry when she hears that you have taken my scarf. She gave it to me herself!"

"Ooh!" said the North Wind. "I didn't

know that. The Fairy Queen, eh? Well, well! Why didn't you tell me that at first?"

"You didn't give me a chance," said the brownie. "You nearly blew me away to the end of the world!"

"Well, I'm very sorry about your scarf," said the North Wind. "As a matter of fact, I did take it! It looked so bright hanging there that I thought I'd like a game with it. So I pulled it off the line and blew it right away."

"Oh dear!" said Heyho. "Do you know where it is now?"

"Well, I left it hanging over Wizard Wimple's chimney," said the North Wind. "It looked very funny there, I can tell you."

"My poor scarf!" groaned Heyho. "Well, you'll have to take me to Wizard Wimple's to get it back, North Wind."

"Easy!" cried the wind, and lifted Heyho up into the air in a trice. He blew him along at a terrific speed and put him down *bump*, just outside Wizard Wimple's cottage. Heyho looked up at the chimney – but alas! There was no yellow scarf there!

"That's funny!" said the North Wind. "Let's ask what he's done with it."

"You go!" said Heyho, nervously. "I'm not very fond of wizards."

So the North Wind banged at the door, and the wizard's black cat answered it.

"Where's the scarf that was hanging over the chimney?" demanded the North Wind.

"So it was you who put it there!" said the cat. "Well, my master was very cross about it. He has given it to Witch Widdershins to make a spell with. She wanted a scarf just like that."

"Oh dear!" cried Heyho in dismay.

"Quick, North Wind, take me to Witch Widdershins before she uses my lovely scarf for her horrid spells."

The North Wind caught up Heyho once more and blew him off to Witch Widdershins' cottage in the middle of a thick wood. He knocked at the door, and the witch looked out of the window.

"What do you want?" she asked crossly.

"The yellow scarf that the wizard gave you," answered the wind. "Have you used it for a spell yet?"

"No," said the witch. "It wasn't quite the right colour after all. So I gave it to Mr Biscuits, the man who sells me my bread. He lives at the other side of the wood."

She banged the window down, and the wind turned to poor Heyho.

"Well, we'd better go to Mr Biscuits," he said. "My, this is a journey, isn't it?"

Off they went again, and soon arrived at Mr Biscuits' shop. He was baking bread, and when he came out to see them he was covered with flour.

"Do you want to buy my loaves?" he asked.

"No," said the wind. "We want that

yellow scarf that Witch Widdershins gave you. It belongs to Heyho."

"Oh, I gave it to my little girl, Cherry Bun," said Mr Biscuits. "She has gone on an errand to Mother Buttercup, up the hill."

"We'll go and meet her," said the wind. So once again Heyho was whisked off. He was put down just by a little girl – but she was not wearing the yellow scarf.

"Is your name Cherry Bun?" asked the North Wind. The little girl nodded. "Well, where's that yellow scarf, little girl?"

"I've g-g-given it to my f-f-friend," said Cherry Bun, rather frightened to see such an enormous person as the North Wind. "The colour didn't suit me, and she gave me a little blue purse in exchange. Would you like that instead?"

She held out the purse, but Heyho shook his head.

"No, I want my scarf," he said. "Where does your friend live?"

"Over there in Higgledy village," said Cherry Bun. So off went the wind and the brownie once more. They soon arrived at Higgledy, and asked for Cherry Bun's friend. When they found her, they looked in vain for the scarf.

"Oh, an elf came by and saw me wearing it, and he said it didn't belong to me, so he took it away," said the little girl, with tears in her eyes. "I don't know where he went to."

Heyho felt like crying too! It seemed as if he never would get his scarf back!

"I'm hungry and tired," said the North Wind. "Let's buy some buns and chocolate, Heyho, and have a picnic."

So they did, and after that they felt

better. Then they hunted all over the countryside for the elf, but couldn't find him.

"Well, I'm really very sorry," said the North Wind. "But I don't see that I can do any more for you, Heyho, except take you home. I'm very tired, and I want to go back and finish my sleep."

So he took Heyho home, and set him down on his own doorstep – and oh dear me, whatever do you think! Why, tied tightly round Heyho's shiny knocker was his lovely yellow scarf! Someone had put it there for him!

100

"Well!" cried the North Wind, crossly. "Here it is after all! And you needn't have woken me up and made me rush round the country like that, after all! I've a good mind to blow you to the end of – "

"Oh, no, you won't," said Heyho. "It was your fault to begin with, North Wind. You just go right back and finish your sleep, and don't be so cross!"

The North Wind puffed Heyho's hat off, and then flew away to his house on the mountain. Heyho picked up his hat, untied his scarf, and went to Twiddle's house to get his key.

"Oh!" said Twiddle when he opened the door. "I'm so glad you're back, Heyho – and you needn't have bothered about your scarf after all! I happened to be walking out today, and I saw a little girl wearing your lovely scarf. So I made her give it to me and brought it back for you – and I expect you found it tied round your door knocker, didn't you?"

"Yes, I did," said Heyho. "Thank you, Twiddle."

He took his key, unlocked his little front door, and made himself a cup of cocoa.

"Well!" he said. "To think I've had all that flying about for nothing! I might just as well have stayed at home and read my new storybook!"

And so he might!

The Dancing
Fox-Kettle

Once upon a time, in far-away Japan, there was an old, old temple. It was falling to pieces but there was no money to build it up again, for the people who lived round about it were very poor.

An old man served in the temple, and he was very much grieved to see his beloved temple gradually tumbling down. But he was even poorer than anybody else, so could do nothing to save it.

Now one day he found that the kettle in which he boiled the water to make tea had a hole in it, so the water all ran out and he could make no tea.

"What shall I do?" he thought. "The hole is too big to mend, and I have no money to buy a new kettle."

Then he suddenly remembered a very old and rusty kettle that had been hanging from one of the beams in the temple ever since he could remember.

"It is old and rusty," he said, "but it may perhaps boil my water for me. I will get it and see."

So he went to get it. He cut it down, and polished it up a little. Then he filled it with water and set it on the fire to boil.

But suddenly, while the kettle stood over the fire, a very strange thing happened.

A fox's head grew out of the spout, the handle turned into a bushy tail, a body covered with reddish-brown fur appeared between them, and four legs grew out at the bottom!

"Bless me!" cried the old man in a fright. "The kettle's turned into a fox. Did anyone ever hear of such a thing!"

The fox suddenly began to leap about in the temple, dancing here and there, springing to and fro, and spinning round and round. The old man watched it in fear.

"Help! Help!" he called. "Here's a kettle that has turned into a fox! Help! Help!"

At once his friends came running in, and were amazed to see the fox leaping about so madly. They chased him and tried to

catch him, but he was too clever for them. He twisted and turned, leaped and sprang, ran and dodged as if he were cat, dog and fox mixed into one.

The men ran round and round after him, tumbling over each other in their haste. At last they caught the fox and dragged him towards a wooden box.

Just as they had taken off the lid and were putting him inside, he turned into a kettle again! His head, tail and legs disappeared, and there he was, just an old, rusty kettle.

Everybody was most surprised.

"Never mind what he is now!" said the old man. "Pack him into the box, for nobody knows what he will turn into next."

So the kettle was put into the box and the lid was tied down.

"We had better throw it into the lake,"

106

said the old man. "A dancing fox-kettle ought not to be in our temple. Leave the box with me and I will drop it into the lake tomorrow!"

So the box with the kettle in was left with the old man. His friends had not been gone very long before someone appeared at the temple door.

It was a tinker, and he called to the old man:

"Will you buy any of my goods – any kettles or pans, silks or slippers?"

"No," said the old man. "I have no money."

"Well, have you anything I could buy from you?" asked the tinker.

The old man suddenly thought of the fox-kettle.

"It would be silly to throw it away if I could perhaps sell it for a few pence," he thought. So he fetched the box from the corner and undid the lid.

"What will you give me for this old kettle?" he asked. "It is quite good for boiling water in."

"It is a poor thing," said the tinker, "but I will give you threepence for it."

"Very well," said the old man. So the tinker gave him threepence, and took the kettle from the box. He slung it on his back, and went off home to his wife, for it was getting late.

They sat down to drink tea, and the tinker told his wife all that had happened during the day.

"I bought that old kettle for three-pence!" he said, showing it to his wife, "but I doubt if it was worth it."

The couple looked at it and saw a strange thing happen – for once more fur grew all over the kettle, a fox's head and tail appeared, and four legs!

Then the fox-kettle sprang up, and began once more to dance and leap about. The tinker and his wife could hardly believe their eyes.

The woman got up to stroke the fox, but straightaway it turned into a kettle again. No sooner had she sat down than it changed once more into a fox, and she tried to catch it. In the twinkle of an eye it became a kettle, and so it went on until the tinker and his wife were tired, and sat down laughing.

"Husband!" said the woman. "There is a fortune in that kettle."

"How?" asked the husband in surprise.

"Well, do you suppose that anyone else in the world has a fox-kettle?" asked the woman. "Think what a lot of money you would make by showing it to people as you go about the country!"

"You are right!" said the man. "I will take it with me tomorrow."

So the next day the tinker set off with the kettle. He went along crying, "Come, see the wonderful fox-kettle! Come see, come see! The only one in the world."

109

Soon a crowd gathered round him and waited to see what would happen. The tinker put the kettle down on the ground, and lo and behold, fur grew all over it, legs, tail and head appeared, and there was a fox frisking all about, darting between the people and back again!

Then all in a moment he turned into an old, rusty kettle again, and lay there on the ground as still as a stone.

"Wonderful! Marvellous! cried the crowd. "Do it again, tinker, do it again!"

"Fill the magic kettle with money first," said the artful tinker. "Then the fox-kettle will perform once more."

The crowd threw money into the kettle, and the tinker emptied it all out into his own bag. No sooner had he put the kettle on the ground again than once more it became covered with fur, grew head, legs and tail, and there was the leaping, darting fox again.

How the crowd laughed and cheered! The tinker took much money that day, and his wife was delighted when he showed her all the money he had got.

Day after day he took the fox-kettle out

on show, and the people who watched filled it with pennies to see it perform. Soon the tinker became rich, and was able to build himself a fine little house and grow a little garden full of flowers.

Now, one day a great nobleman heard of the magic fox-kettle and thought it would be a fine thing to have it at a grand party he was giving. So he sent a messenger to the tinker and asked him to come, and to bring his wonderful kettle with him.

The tinker went. He was very nervous

when he saw such a lot of grand gentlemen and ladies, and he hoped the fox-kettle would perform well.

He put it on the ground as usual. It had not lain there for many moments before reddish fur grew all over it, and a fox's head grew out of the spout. The handle turned into a fine bushy tail, and four legs appeared at the bottom of the kettle. Then, with a spring into the air, the fox began to do his usual dance, leaping and bounding all over the place, to the marvel and delight of the company.

"Wonderful!" they said, amazed. "It is wonderful! Never have we seen such a thing before."

Suddenly the fox stopped his dance and lay down on the ground. His tail, head and legs disappeared, and the fur vanished. Only a rusty old kettle could be seen.

"Let us see it again!" they all cried.

"If it please your gracious and most generous honours," said the tinker, "the kettle likes to be filled with money before it performs again."

All the grand company drew out their purses and threw gold into the kettle.

Never before had it been filled with such valuable money, and when it was full to the brim, and running over, the tinker reached down to empty it into his bag.

But hey presto! Before he could do that the kettle suddenly turned into a fox again, and with one great bound jumped right over the heads of the company and disappeared down the hillside!

"Stop him! I say stop him!" shouted the tinker. "He has all my lovely gold money!"

But nobody could stop the fox, for he had gone too far. Although the company waited and waited he didn't come back and the tinker at last had to go home to his fine new house without his fox-kettle.

The fox ran on until he came to the little temple in which the old man had first found him as a kettle. He ran in, and there was the same old man dusting round as usual.

"Bless us!" cried the man in astonishment. "What is a fox doing here?"

As he spoke the fox lay down at his feet, and turned into a rusty old kettle.

"Bless us again!" cried the old man. "If it isn't that fox-kettle I sold to the tinker! Now whatever has he come back to me for?"

He stooped down to pick the kettle up, but it was so heavy that he could not lift it. He took off the lid to see what was inside, and saw that it was filled to the brim with gold pieces.

"A miracle!" he cried. "The fox-kettle

has brought us gold to rebuild our beloved temple! Come, everyone, and see!"

All his friends crowded round and marvelled. There was indeed enough money to restore the temple and make it beautiful again. The gold pieces were all emptied out, and the old man spent them well. As for the kettle, it was hung up in its old place on a beam in the roof.

On the day that the temple was finished, and everyone had come to see it and pray in it, a curious thing happened.

The kettle jumped off its string, turned into a fox, ran round and round the temple in delight, threw up its tail and galloped out on the hillside.

Everyone watched him go in astonishment – but nobody ever saw him come back – for from that day to this the magic fox-kettle has never been seen again!

A Surprising
Afternoon

For four days Kitty and John had been excited whenever they had thought of Saturday.

"We're going to a party then," Kitty told everyone. "It will be a wonderful party, with a magician and a Punch and Judy show. Aren't we lucky?"

And then, do you know, on Saturday morning poor Kitty woke up with a bad cold! Did you ever know anything so disappointing?

"Darling, I'm afraid you can't go to the party," said her mother. "John has no cold at all, so I will keep you away from him, and he can go. But you certainly can't."

"I won't give my cold to them. I promise I won't," said poor Kitty. "I'll keep it all to myself, really I will."

But it was no good. Mother said she

must stay indoors that day. "You can play with all your dolls and toys in your bedroom," she said. "John must keep downstairs in the living-room, away from you. I don't want him to catch it as well."

Kitty began to sob and cry. Really, she had never been so disappointed in all her life.

Her mother was upset too. "Kitty dear," she said, "I am very, very sorry about it. So is John. He says if you really feel unhappy he will give up going to the party too. But I know you wouldn't want him to do that."

"No, I wouldn't," said Kitty, drying her eyes, and then beginning to cry all over again. "But oh, Mummy, it's so dreadful to lie here and think of that lovely party."

"Kitty, I would be so proud of you if you could be brave about it," said her mother. "I hate to see you unhappy, so don't make me feel sad too, will you?"

Well, Kitty loved her mother very much, so she made up her mind she wouldn't cry – at least, not when Mummy was in the room. She didn't want to be brave at all. She just wanted to be horrid and miserable and sniffy. But after all, when you love

somebody you want them to be proud of you, so Kitty decided she'd try.

She lay in bed with her doll and a book, sniffing hard. The sun shone in at her window and made her blink. She had some blackcurrant lozenges to suck and they were very nice. She looked round at her toys, and they all seemed to look back at her as if they were sorry about the party.

John popped his head in at the bedroom door before he went to the party. "Goodbye, Kitty!" he said. "I'll bring you back a balloon if I can!"

That made Kitty feel unhappy again,

119

but she managed to smile at John. Good old John – fancy saying he wouldn't go to the party if it made her unhappy to think of him there without her!

Kitty's mother had made her comfortable and told her to have a sleep that afternoon. Then she would forget about the party. So Kitty lay there, feeling rather sleepy, watching the sun that came through the pretty net curtains. She looked round the room. She stared at her toys, and she stared at a little hole in the wall, thinking how once Mummy had said that a mouse had popped out from it and looked at her while she sat there sewing.

And then a very strange and peculiar thing happened. Really, Kitty could hardly believe her eyes!

From the hole came a crowd of tiny men, no bigger than mice! As Kitty looked she saw that some little women were there too, and one of them was pushing a pram with a very tiny baby in it! There were some small children, like running dolls, scampering beside the women!

And then an even stranger thing happened! The teddy bear, who sat in a doll's armchair, suddenly got up and went over to the little people! Kitty lay and stared in amazement. She was so astonished that she couldn't even sit up!

"Good afternoon," said the teddy bear in a low voice. "You'd better all go back home. John went to a party, but Kitty has a cold. She's here, in the bedroom. Shhh!"

The little people looked round, scared. They saw Kitty's bed, and Kitty on it. They began to chatter in tiny voices like the sound of swallows.

"We'll go back! Is she asleep? She mustn't see us!"

Then one of the children began to cry.

"But you said we might have a party here with the toys – you did, you did! You said the children would be gone and we could all come and play!"

"Shh! Shh!" said everyone, looking at Kitty to see if she was asleep or awake.

The little girl knew at once what the toys had been going to do. They had meant to have their friends to tea while she and John were out! And their friends must belong to the fairy-folk, for they were so very small.

She sat up. The little people at once ran to the hole, and the teddy bear looked really frightened.

"Teddy, don't let them go home," begged Kitty. "Tell them to stay. I'd love to see them. Quick, catch them! They are the dearest little people I have ever seen. Do, do have them to tea with you. I promise

I won't get out of bed. I told Mummy I wouldn't – so I shan't frighten any of you, you see."

Teddy smiled and ran to the little folk, who were squeezing into the hole as fast as they could go. He whispered to them, and they came slowly back, staring at Kitty, and smiling shyly.

And then all the other toys got busy too! Goodness, it was quite a shock to Kitty to see her doll, which she had in bed with her, slip out of the sheets and run over to her tiny friends. She picked the baby out of the pram and kissed it.

"How is the darling?" she said. That was the first time Kitty had ever heard her doll speak, and she was pleased to hear what a sweet voice she had.

The other bears, one brown and one white, shook hands with the little people. The three small dolls in the dolls'-house came running out of the front door with tiny shouts of welcome. The blue rabbit lollopped over, and the brown dog wuffed round the children, who patted him in

delight. Mickey Mouse wheeled the pram away and put it into the little garage that belonged to the toy motor-cars.

The teddy bear came over to Kitty's bed and looked at her rather timidly. "Are you sure you don't mind if we have a party while you are in bed?" he asked. "You see, it's the baby's birthday, and so, when we knew you and John were going to a party, we thought that we would give one too."

"Of course I don't mind. It's simply lovely," said Kitty happily. "Go on, Teddy, do everything you want to. I shan't mind. Use my sweets out of my toy sweetshop, too, for the tiny little children. And tell the dolls'-house dolls to cook on the stove, if they want to."

Well, after that the party went on merrily. The dolls'-house dolls had already baked cakes in the oven of the stove. Teddy fetched a bottle of sweets from the toy sweetshop and gave one each to the children. They squealed with delight, and waved their tiny little hands to Kitty.

"Let's have our party where Kitty can see us," said Angela, her doll. "She's so kind and nice, she'd love to watch us."

So they took the two dolls' tables and all the dolls' chairs and stools and arranged them just where Kitty could see them. The children all sat down, and Angela, the doll, had the little baby on her knee. She was very fond of it.

The dolls'-house dolls had made some lovely cakes! They set them out on the plates belonging to Kitty's tea set. Angela gave the baby to the blue rabbit for a moment and came over to Kitty.

"You won't mind if we use the tea set you had at Christmas-time, will you?" she said. "We won't break anything."

"I would love you to use it," Kitty said generously. It was lovely to watch tea being made in the little blue teapot, and milk being poured into the blue milk-jug. Sugar was put in the sugar-basin, and one of the dolls cut a whole plateful of bread and butter for the children. You should have seen the slices! They were only as big as slices of cucumber!

There was a birthday cake too, iced all over with pink, and there was a tiny candle on it for the baby, who was one that day! The white bear lit the candle.

Kitty thought she had never seen such a pretty little birthday cake in her life.

Presently Angela put two pieces of bread and butter and jam on a plate, with a tiny chocolate bun, a currant bun, three tiny biscuits, and a slice of the pink birthday

cake. She carried the plate over to Kitty's bed and smiled at her.

"Could you eat these?" she said. "I expect you don't feel very hungry as you have a cold, but we would like you to have a bit of the party!"

"Oooh!" Kitty said, in delight. "Of course I could eat this! It all looks most delicious. And I'd like a cup of your tea too, if you've got some to spare."

So the little girl sat up in bed and ate the tiny cakes and biscuits and bread and butter, and drank a cup of the toys' tea. It *was* most delicious. As for the birthday cake, it melted in Kitty's mouth. She watched the baby blow out the candle. It was a lovely birthday party!

The three little dolls'-house dolls cleared away the tea-things after that, and the little people began to play games. They asked Kitty if she would set the cassette player going for them to play musical chairs, and she said she would. So the teddy bear gave it to her on her bed, and she put a tape in while the toys set out a long row of chairs and stools.

"Will you stop it when you like?" asked

Angela. So Kitty started the tune, and then after a while stopped it suddenly. There was a wild scramble for chairs. The teddy bear didn't get one, so he had to stand out. Then Kitty set the music going again, and stopped it when she liked. It was fun to watch the toys and the little people playing!

The blue rabbit won that game, and he got a new pink ribbon to tie round his neck for a prize. He was very proud. Then they played blindman's buff, and Kitty nearly fell out of bed in excitement when the brown bear got caught behind the curtain by the biggest of the little people.

Soon Teddy brought out a whole bunch of small coloured balloons for the little folk to play with. They were so tiny! They were not much bigger than peas, but they were just the right size for the tiny children. The brown bear came over to Kitty's bed and gave her one too.

It was like a tiny coloured bubble. Kitty was so delighted. Then the toys brought out a small bran-tub full of parcels, and every guest had to dip his or her hand in

and get a surprise. Oh, the shouts and squeals when the parcels were undone, and the little folk found toys and brooches and other presents!

Angela and Teddy carried the tub over to Kitty's bed. "Would you like a dip in the tub?" asked Teddy. "It was so nice of you to let us have this party."

Kitty dipped a finger and thumb into the tub. Her hand was far too big to put in. She drew out a little, long, thin parcel and undid it. Inside was – what do you think? A tiny silver wand, no bigger than a needle!

"That's a little magic wand," said Angela, excited. "You are lucky, Kitty. Keep it safe, won't you? You can do magic with that!"

Suddenly the front door banged downstairs. It was John back from the party! At once all the toys rushed about in a great bustle. The tables and chairs were whisked away. The baby was put into its pram. The children were kissed goodbye.

Then all the little folk waved to Kitty and squeezed hurriedly into the hole. They were gone! The toys sat down on chairs and shelves, and the dolls'-house dolls went into the dolls'-house and shut the door. When John opened the bedroom door and popped in his head, there wasn't a movement to be seen.

"Hello, Kitty!" said John. "I'm back! There was a fine magician. He did all kinds of magic. And I've got a balloon for you! Hope it wasn't too dull for you. Mummy says you haven't had any tea. She says she peeped in at four o'clock, and she thinks you were asleep. So she'll bring you up a nice supper now."

"John, I've had tea, and I've been to a party too!" said Kitty. "I've got a balloon – and a present out of a bran-tub! It's a

magic silver wand! I don't mind missing the party you went to, not one bit, because I've been to a much more exciting one! Come and see my wand."

"I mustn't come right into the room in case I get your cold," said John. "I'll see it tomorrow. But I think you've been asleep, Kitty!"

"Well, I haven't!" said Kitty. "Because I've got a tiny little balloon and the magic wand. I'll do some magic tomorrow, and you'll know I'm telling the truth. I'm glad I missed the party!"

John went to bed, puzzled and excited. Tomorrow Kitty will show him the things she was given at her party – and I wonder what magic she will do with that wand, don't you?

The Galloping
Seahorse

Once upon a time a very strange thing happened to Janet. She was having a holiday by the sea, and she was fishing in the rock-pools to see if she could get some shrimps for tea.

She pushed her net along the sand, and then lifted it up to see what she had got in it. There were no shrimps – no little crabs – no fish – but there was something else!

There was a baby mermaid! You know what mermaids are, don't you? – pretty creatures that live in the sea, with heads and arms like those we have, but tails like fishes!

Well, Janet stared at the baby mermaid in her net in great surprise. "Are you a sea-fairy?" she asked. "You do look odd with your little fish-tail!"

"I'm a little mermaid!" said the tiny

creature in a voice like the splash of a wave. "I was asleep under a stone, and now you've caught me!"

"I shall show you to my friends," said Janet, excited.

"No, please don't!" begged the little mermaid. "I don't want you to. I'm very shy. It is horrid to meet a lot of strange people if you are shy."

Now it so happened that Janet was shy too, so she knew just how the mermaid felt. It is a horrid feeling to be shy, isn't it?

"Well, if you feel like that, I will put

you back in your pool again," Janet said kindly. That was nice of her, wasn't it? She put her net down into the water carefully, and watched the mermaid swim out of it just like a tiny fish. She disappeared under a stone.

"Well, that was very strange!" said Janet. "I've never seen a mermaid before."

Now the next day Janet went to bathe with her friends, and they had a floating rubber bed. It was fun to climb on it and lie down. Janet climbed up too when her turn came, and liked to feel the funny floating bed bobbing up and down on the waves.

The other children began playing with a ball, throwing it to one another. They forgot about Janet and the floating bed. Janet lay flat on her back, looking up into the blue sky. It was lovely.

But do you know, the sea took the bed away, and the wind helped to blow it along – so that when Janet sat up again, she found that she was right out at sea! The beach was ever so far away – and she could hardly hear the shouts of the children playing in the waves with their ball.

Janet was frightened. Suppose she fell off into the deep sea? She could swim a little but not much. She didn't know what to do. It wasn't any good shouting, because she was too far away from the shore for any one to hear.

The little girl looked round her to see

if a rowing-boat was near. But no – not a single boat was to be seen. The sea took her farther and farther away as she sat up, wondering what to do.

Janet began to cry. She rubbed her eyes but the tears rolled down her cheeks fast. And then suddenly a funny thing happened!

Just by the bed a tiny head popped up! And whose head do you suppose it was? Can you guess? Yes – it was the head of the little mermaid that Janet had caught in her net the day before. Just think of that!

"What are you crying for?" asked the mermaid, scrambling up on the floating bed.

"Oh, hello, mermaid!" said Janet. "I'm so pleased to see you. I'm lost on the sea and I don't know what to do."

"Good gracious!" said the mermaid. "What a dreadful thing to happen! You should have been more careful. Now, let me see if I can help you. Wait a minute – I must think."

Janet stared at the tiny creature while she thought hard.

"Can you ride a horse?" the mermaid asked suddenly.

Janet thought that was a very strange thing to ask just then. She nodded her head. "Yes," she said. "I can ride my cousin's pony. I know how to ride. Why?"

"Well, that's all right then," said the mermaid. "I can get you one of the white

139

horses we keep here in the sea. You can ride it back to the beach."

"White horses!" said Janet in surprise. "What do you mean?"

"Well, haven't you heard people say, when the sea is rather rough, 'Look! There are white horses today'?" asked the mermaid.

"Yes, but I thought they just meant the white curling-over bit of the waves," said Janet. "I thought those were the white horses."

"So they are," said the mermaid. "Those white curling pieces are the manes of our white horses. Sometimes they go for a gallop under the sea, and make the sea nice and rough. Their manes just show over the top of the water. Now, I can get you safely back home, but you must never float on the rubber bed again. It's too dangerous; there might not be anyone to help you."

"What will happen to the floating bed?" asked Janet.

"I'll take care of that," said the mermaid. "I and my brothers and sisters will see that the tide takes it to your beach tomorrow, so look for it there. Now I'm just going to get your white horse."

She dived into the sea. In a minute or two she was back, leading a fine white horse whose curly mane showed just above the water. The horse put its head out and neighed to Janet.

"Slip off the bed on to his back," said the mermaid. "He's very gentle. Hold on to his mane when he gallops."

Janet slid off the bed on to the horse's broad back. "Goodbye!" called the mermaid from the bed. The horse began to gallop. It was grand fun!

Janet held on to his curly white mane very tightly. Nearer and nearer to the shore they galloped. Janet wanted to shout for joy!

Just as they got into shallow water the horse stopped. Janet slipped off his back and patted his nose. He turned and galloped back. Janet could see his curly mane going farther and farther out to sea.

"Where's the bed – where's the bed?" cried the children, running to Janet.

They hadn't seen the horse at all. Janet told them her adventure but they didn't believe her.

"You're a naughty girl, you've lost the bed!" they cried. "We don't believe your story."

"The mermaid will bring it back to our beach tomorrow," said Janet. "She promised, but she said we shouldn't float on it any more."

"Well, we'll believe you if we get our bed back," said the children.

And do you think the floating bed came back? Yes – it did! There it was the next morning, put safely on the sand for the children. So they will have to believe Janet, won't they!

A Hole in
Santa's Sack

One Christmas-time the green goblins thought it would be a fine idea to follow Santa Claus and cut a hole in his sack. Then, maybe, some toys would fall out and they would have a fine time playing with them.

So they laid their plans, and on Christmas Eve they followed Santa Claus when he dashed through the sky on his sleigh. The bells jingled, and the reindeer tossed their big heads as they galloped over the clouds. Santa Claus sang a rollicking song as he went, and down below people said, "Dear me, someone's got their television on very loud tonight!"

The green goblins had a small aeroplane, and when Santa Claus landed on a roof they landed too – but behind a chimney pot so that they shouldn't be seen. They crept out of their plane and peeped to see what Santa was doing. He had put his sack down and was tying his reindeer up to a big chimney.

"Now's our chance," said the green goblins. "Who has the scissors?"

"I have," said the biggest goblin. He ran up to the sack and snipped a hole in it. Then he ran quickly back behind the chimney as Santa Claus turned to pick up his sack. Whistling softly, the jolly old man

slipped down the chimney. The goblins heard something fall from his sack as he hoisted it up on his shoulder.

When Santa Claus was safely down the chimney the goblins ran to see what had fallen out. It was a large red box!

"What is it?" cried the goblin. "Oh, it must be full of toys! How lovely! It must be full of toys!"

They popped the box behind a chimney and waited for Santa Claus to come up again. They thought maybe he would drop something else out of the hole in his sack. But what a disappointment for them! When old Santa came up from the chimney the goblins saw that he had found the hole and had pinned it up with a large safety-pin!

Santa Claus spoke crossly to his reindeer.

"Do you know, I found a big hole in my sack just now, reindeer? I've told you before that you are not to nibble my sack!"

Then he got into his sleigh and drove away. The green goblins looked at one another.

"It's no good going after him now," said

the biggest one. "He won't drop any more toys tonight."

"Well, it doesn't matter," said the smallest goblin, in his high voice. "We've got a whole box of toys, haven't we? By the weight of it there will be enough for all of us! Come on, let's go home."

So they all crowded into their aeroplane and flew to their dark little cave in the green mountains. They ran the aeroplane into its shed, opened their cave-door and hopped inside, pulling the box with them. My, it certainly was heavy for those small goblins to pull!

They shut the door. They lit three candles and looked at the box.

"It's got a catch here," said the biggest goblin. "If two of us push hard, we can get it out of the loop it is in. Oh, I wonder if there's a doll inside? If there is, I shall have it!"

"And I shall have an engine if there is one there!" said another.

"And I shall have a humming-top!" said a third.

"And I shall have a book," said the smallest.

"Come and help me to undo the box," said the biggest one. "It's very stiff, this catch."

Two of them pushed at the catch – and suddenly it slipped back. The lid of the box flew open and out shot an enormous jack-in-the-box, much bigger than the goblins themselves, jerking about on his long spring in a very curious manner.

"Eee-eee-eee!" said the jack-in-the-box, nodding his grinning head at the

frightened goblins. "Eee-eee-eee!"

"Ooo-ooo-ooo!" squealed the goblins, tumbling over one another, trying to get away. "What is it? What is it?"

"Eee-eee-eee!" said the jack-in-the-box, nodding and grinning in delight. "I'm glad you are frightened of me! Children are never frightened of jack-in-the-boxes nowadays! But I'm pleased to scare nasty

149

little robbers like you! Eee-eee-eee!"

The goblins tore out of their cave as fast as they could. The jack-in-the-box laughed till he cried. A rabbit who was passing by heard him and looked into the cave.

"Good gracious!" said the rabbit. "What are you?"

"A jack-in-the-box, quite harmless!" said the jack. And he told the rabbit all about how the goblins had cut a hole in Santa's sack, and made his box tumble out. He told the rabbit too how frightened they

had been when he jumped out at them!

"It serves them right!" said the rabbit, grinning. "Those goblins are a perfect nuisance! They steal and they tell stories and they scare all the little mice and hedgehogs they meet. It's a good thing someone has come along to scare them!"

"What am I going to do?" said the jack-in-the-box. "I should really live in a house and amuse the children. But now I shall have no home and amuse no one."

"Well, I have eight small bunnies who would love to have you," said the rabbit. "Come and live with us. You don't need anything to eat, do you? We will look after you and you shall jump in and out as much as you like."

"Oh, thank you very much," said the jack-in-the-box, delighted. "Push me down into my box, please, rabbit; shut the lid, and fasten the catch. Then you can easily carry me down your burrow."

So off to the rabbit's home went the merry jack-in-the-box, and dear me, how he made the young rabbits laugh when he popped in and out at them, shouting "Eee-eee-eee!" in his funny high voice!

And do you know what the mother rabbit does sometimes, when the green goblins have been very bad? She takes the jack-in-the-box and hides him under a bush or by a big toadstool – and when those goblins come running by, the jack-in-the-box jumps out at them with a rush!

"Eee-eee-eee," he cries, and nods about on his long, springy neck. And those goblins squeal in fright and go tumbling over and over on the grass, trying to get away. One day they'll pack up and leave their cave, and then everyone on the hill will be very pleased. Good old jack-in-the-box!

Mister Dear-Me's
Handkerchief

Mister Dear-Me had a very bad memory. He was always forgetting things. Mrs Dear-Me said he had no memory at all, only a forgettery, and it seemed as if she was right.

"Now listen to me, Dear-Me," she said one day. "I'm going out to tea this afternoon. I want you to remember four things. Please put the kettle on to make a cup of tea for yourself at four o'clock. Please give the cat its milk. Please put out the laundry for the van to pick up after tea. And please keep the dog out of the kitchen, or he will spoil my nice new cushions."

"Certainly, my dear, I'll remember all those things," said Dear-Me. "Look – I have such a good idea. I will tie four knots in my handkerchief – this knot shall be for the kettle. This one shall be for the cat, so that I shall not forget its milk. And this knot shall remind me to put out the washing. And this one will tell me to keep the dog out of the kitchen. There! Four big knots in my handkerchief! I shall certainly remember everything now!"

"Well, see you do!" said Mrs Dear-Me, and off she went in her best hat to have tea with her friend Sally Dimple.

Mister Dear-Me put his handkerchief into his pocket and read the paper for some time. Soon he felt as if he wanted to sneeze, so he took his handkerchief out of his pocket in case – for he had good manners, and he always sneezed into his handkerchief.

He saw the four knots and at first he was so surprised that he quite forgot to sneeze.

"Dear, dear me!" said Mister Dear-Me. "Look at those four knots! Four things to remember! Whatever in the wide world did I have to remember?"

He sat and thought hard.

"There was a knot for the kettle," he said at last. "And a knot for the cat. And a

knot for – for – for – oh yes, for the laundry
– and a knot for the dog!"

He looked at the four knots and frowned.
"The worst of it is," he said, "I don't know
which knot was for which, I really don't.
I'm afraid I shall get everything mixed up
now, because I can't imagine which knot I
did for the kettle, which one is for the cat,
and which for the other things."

Poor Mister Dear-Me! He did try so hard
to remember the four things he had to do.
He kept fingering the knots and pulling
at them. Then he suddenly heard the dog
whining outside the door.

"Ah yes! I had to give something some

milk," he said. "Wait a minute, Wuff-Wuff. I will get you a dish of milk!"

Mister Dear-Me hurried to get the milk and poured out a big bowlful for Wuff-Wuff. He let the dog in and Wuff-Wuff joyfully drank every drop of it. Then he jumped up on to Mrs Dear-Me's chair, and settled himself to sleep on the nice new cushions.

"Good!" said Mister Dear-Me to himself. "That's one knot remembered. I'll untie it."

He untied it and thought hard as he looked at the next knot. "Something had to be put outside the door," he said at last. "What was it? Ah! The kettle! Good!"

So he set the kettle outside the back door and undid the second knot. He was pleased. Then he saw the cat come mewing in at the door and he shooshed her out. "No, no!" he said. "That was another thing I had to remember, Puss. Not to let you in, in case you dirtied Mrs Dear-Me's nice new cushions. Shoo!"

So the poor cat had to go outside, though she was longing for her milk. Mister Dear-Me undid the third knot and stared hard at the last one. "I know! I know!" he cried. "It was the laundry. Put it on to boil at four o'clock! Oh, how clever I am, to be sure!"

He took the basket of washing, emptied it into the big boiler, poured water into it, and set it on the stove. He undid the last knot, and felt very proud of himself.

"Just see what knots in a handkerchief

will do!" he said. "I've remembered everything!"

At six o'clock he opened the door to Mrs Dear-Me with a beaming smile. "I remembered everything!" he said.

Mrs Dear-Me kissed him and then stood still in surprise. "What's that odd bubbling noise?" she said.

"That's the washing, boiling on the stove, dear," said Mister Dear-Me. "You told me to put it on at four o'clock."

"Oh my!" said Mrs Dear-Me, and she rushed to the kitchen. There she saw the dog asleep on her cushions, the washing boiling to nothing on the stove, the cat outside trying to get in at the window – and no kettle anywhere!

"Shoo!" said Mrs Dear-Me to the dog. "Come in, poor Puss-cat! Oh, land's sake, here's the kettle outside the back door! Did you think the laundry van would pick it up and take it away to wash and iron, Dear-Me? And oh, my poor washing on the stove! Here are your socks boiled to bits! And your nice flannel trousers shrunk to shorts! And your nice flannel shirts would just about fit a doll! Dear-

Me, I am just going to whack you with your own walking-stick till you begin to remember a few things just a bit better than this, next time!"

But Dear-Me had remembered something and was nowhere to be seen. He had remembered how very unpleasant Mrs Dear-Me could be when she was angry. He had remembered that he didn't like to be with her when she was in a temper. He had remembered that the tool-shed was a good place to hide in. And he had remembered that he had better go before she looked round to find him!

So you see he could remember four things quite well without any knots in his handkerchief. Poor Mister Dear-Me – he's probably sitting in the tool-shed still!

The
Runaway Hat

It all happened because the wind blew Jill's hat off. It blew so hard that her straw hat flew off her head and went bowling over and over down the hill.

"Run after it, Jill!" said Auntie Kate. "Quick, or it will be lost!"

Jill ran after it, and soon got up to the rolling hat. For a moment it lay still, but just as Jill stooped to pick it up, the wind gave a puff, and sent the hat on again.

What was more annoying still, Jill felt absolutely certain she heard a chuckling laugh, right by her ear.

She looked round. No, nobody was near! Who had laughed, then? Surely it couldn't have been the wind!

She ran on again after her hat. It was bowling on, far in front of her, jumping over puddles as if it knew it mustn't go into them. Then it lay still again.

"Well!" said Jill. "I'll get you this time," and she ran on as fast as she could. She bent down to her hat and caught hold of the brim – but, "Oh botheration!" said Jill – for the wind jerked the hat out of her hand and sent it flying into the wood at the side of the road. And by her ear came that gurgling chuckle again! Just as if somebody were laughing till the tears ran down his cheeks.

Jill looked all round. No one was near.

"All right," said Jill. "I can hear you, Mister Wind! It's jolly mean of you to take away my hat, but I'm going to catch it, so there!" She ran into the wood and looked about for her hat. Yes, there it was, caught in a branch of a tree.

"I'm sure I can climb that!" said Jill, and looked for an easy place to get up.

But would you believe it! No sooner was she climbing up than the wind blew the hat off the branch and sent it down on the ground again. It really was most tiresome.

Jill climbed down. The hat lay away in the distance, half buried in last year's leaves. Jill decided to stalk it, as a cat stalks a bird.

"I believe the hat is helping the wind to tease me!" she thought.

So she dodged from tree to tree until she had nearly reached the heap of dead leaves where she thought the hat lay.

Then suddenly out she pounced and caught hold of it.

But it wasn't the hat! It was a great white toadstool that broke in her hands! Jill heard the wind laugh again and saw the hat running away in front of her.

Jill was growing cross. On she went again, determined not to stop running until she caught that hat. She was quickly catching it up. She would soon have it – two or three steps more – a grab – and oh!

The hat had rolled right into a little pond that lay hidden in a dip in the wood. There it floated, upside down, green with weed and brown with mud.

"Very well," said Jill. "You're a very silly hat. I shall leave you there alone. I'm sure I don't want to wear you any more!"

She thought she heard a laugh behind her. Yes, there it was again, farther off, beyond the near-by trees.

"I'll go and catch that rascally wind if I can!" thought Jill, and went in the direction of the laugh.

Now and again she heard the chuckling, and each time she ran in the direction it came from. After a while she stood still. She could hear no laughing. The wind was gone.

But hark! What was that contented humming sound? Jill listened. Then she stole towards the hazel-trees in front of her, and peeped round them.

What she saw made her stare as if she could not believe her eyes.

She saw a beautiful little glade, full of wild white anemones, each with dainty little frills of green. And they were dancing, every one of them – nodding and swaying, shaking out their little green frills and looking as pretty as a picture.

And kneeling down among them was the wind! He was blowing here and blowing there, making the flowers dance for him in every corner.

Jill watched for a minute. Then she said,

"Mister Wind! Do you know what you have done to my hat?"

The wind turned round in surprise.

"Hello! Why, it's Jill!" He smiled. "Yes, I blew your hat off for a joke!"

"Well, it's rolled into the pond, and I can't wear it any more," said Jill. "I think it's unkind of you."

"Oh dear! Oh dear!" said the wind. "I didn't mean to do that! I must have blown too hard! I'm really very sorry."

"I don't mind a joke," said Jill. "I think jokes are funny, even when they're played on me – but to lose my hat altogether isn't a joke, I can tell you."

"Well, I'd give you my hat to make up for it," said the wind, looking very worried, "only I haven't got one. My brother, the North Wind, blew it away the other day. Would you accept a few of my flowers instead? They're the only ones out, you know, and this is my special garden."

"They are certainly out very early," said Jill. "Yes, I'd like some, please. They'll make up for losing my hat."

The wind picked her a lovely bunch of the dainty little anemones, told her the way out of the wood, laughed, and vanished.

Jill went back up the hill to her auntie. She showed her the flowers.

"Good gracious, Jill!" she cried. "Wherever did you find those flowers? I've never seen them out so early in the year before! How perfectly lovely!"

"The wind sent my hat into a pond," said Jill, "and gave me these flowers to make up for it. What are they called, Auntie Kate?"

167

"They're wood anemones," said Auntie Kate. "But people always call them windflowers, because they dance so prettily in the wind."

"So that's why he's got his garden full of them!" said Jill to herself. "They're his very own flowers! No wonder they dance so prettily when he blows."

And I think when you see the windflowers nodding and swaying when the South Wind blows, you will say too that there couldn't be a better name for the little dancing flowers of the spring.

Belinda
All Alone

Mollie had been playing in the garden
with her teddy bear and her doll. She took
them right down to the bottom where the
wall was, and played with them there.
She climbed into the old pear-tree and sat
on a smooth branch, pulling the teddy up
beside her, but she put Belinda, the doll,
on the top of the wall.

"You might get your clean clothes dirty
if you sit in the tree," she said. "Teddy
hasn't any clothes to get dirty."

Just as she was swinging Teddy up and
down on the branch, her mother called
her.

"Mollie! Here is Auntie Juliet come to
see you!"

Mollie jumped down from the tree
in excitement for she loved her Auntie

Juliet. She took Teddy with her but she forgot all about poor Belinda, who was left sitting on the top of the wall all by herself.

And, oh dear me, Mollie didn't think of poor Belinda again that day! She forgot all about her, and not even when she put her toys away and went to bed did she think of Belinda sitting all alone on the top of the garden wall.

But the toys in the toy cupboard missed her.

"Where is Belinda?" asked the panda, looking all round.

"Oh! She must still be on the garden wall," said the teddy bear, remembering.

"Mollie left her there when she ran to see her Aunt Juliet. She took me with her, but she left Belinda behind."

"Good gracious!" said the clown doll, in surprise. "Poor old Belinda! She will be dreadfully cold and frightened sitting there by herself all night. And supposing she fell off. She might break her leg."

The toys looked at one another in dismay. They all liked Belinda, who was very cheerful and merry, and they couldn't bear to think of her lonely and cold.

"Shall we go and fetch her?" asked the teddy, after a while. "I don't mind going, if someone else will come with me."

"It's so dark," said the clown, looking out of the window.

"I'd be afraid something would catch me and eat me," said the wooden soldier, shivering.

"Well, something might catch and eat Belinda!" said the teddy. "That would be dreadful. Come on, somebody! Who will go with me?"

"I will," said a small voice.

Everyone looked to see who it was. It was the little clockwork mouse! He was a very timid little creature, but Belinda had once stroked him and he had never forgotten it.

"All right," said the teddy. "Come on."

"Wind me up first," said the tiny mouse. "I can't go unless I'm wound up."

So the clown wound him up and he and the teddy bear started out together. They crept out of the window and slid down the drainpipe outside. The little mouse landed on his nose, but he said he wasn't hurt so they went on again.

It was dark – very dark! The teddy walked straight into a flower tub and bumped his head hard. The little mouse rubbed the bump for him and then they went on once more.

Suddenly a great creature pushed by them, and Teddy felt a sharp prick.

"Ooh! Something has stabbed me!" he cried. "It's an enemy with a sword!"

The mouse squeaked in dismay, and the big creature stopped. They could just see its eyes glinting.

"I shan't hurt you," it said. "I'm only a harmless hedgehog, hunting for beetles. You haven't seen any, I suppose?"

"No," said the teddy bear. "I say – what did you stab me with?"

"Oh, one of my prickles must have pricked you," said the hedgehog. "I'm very sorry. Well, if you see any beetles, send them my way, please!"

Off he went again, and the teddy bear started on his way once more. But the little mouse called to him:

"Teddy! You'll have to wind me up again. I've run down!"

So Teddy wound him up and then he ran beside him on his little wheels. They went on towards the bottom of the garden, and oh my, whatever was this that suddenly swooped down on them? It picked the clockwork mouse up in its claws, but Teddy caught hold of him and shouted loudly, "Let go, let go!"

"Hello, who are you?" said a surprised voice. "I am a brown owl."

"I'm a teddy bear," said the teddy. "Please let my friend go. He's not a real mouse, only a clockwork one."

"Is that so?" said the owl, and his big,

round eyes looked closely at the frightened little mouse. "So he is! Well, I don't like the taste of clockwork mice, so I'll let him go. I'm hunting real mice. If you meet any, send them my way, will you?"

He flew up into the air with a soft, feathery sound and the two toys went on their way once more. The teddy trod on a slug and slipped over, and the mouse ran into a big snail and had to be wound up again, but they had no more adventures before they reached the garden wall.

"Belinda! Belinda! Are you there?" called the teddy.

"Oh, Teddy, is it you?" came Belinda's little voice. "Oh, I'm so frightened! There's a great big face looking at me over this wall, and I'm dreadfully afraid. Have you come to rescue me?"

"Yes, and the clockwork mouse is with me," said the teddy bear. "I'll climb up the pear-tree and come and fetch you. The mouse can keep guard at the bottom."

Belinda heard the teddy climbing up the pear-tree and soon he was beside her. He put his arm round her and hugged her.

"Don't be frightened any more," he said.

"We'll take you home safely."

"Look at that great shining face staring at us through those trees," whispered Belinda. "I'm so frightened of it. Do you think it will eat us?"

"I hope not," said the teddy, looking at

the big round face and shivering all down his back. "Come on quickly while there's time!"

He helped Belinda down the tree, and they soon came to where the clockwork mouse was waiting.

"Wind me up again," he said. "I've run down."

But, oh dear me, something had gone wrong with his clockwork and the key seemed dreadfully stiff. It took ages and ages to wind him. And all of a sudden Belinda gave a shriek and pointed upwards.

"There's that horrid face looking at us again!" she said. Sure enough it was! It was peeping over the wall now, and the teddy bear didn't like it a bit.

"We must run!" he said. "Come on, mouse, you're wound up enough now. Take my hand, Belinda."

They hurried up the garden, and except for once when the mouse fell into a puddle and had to be wound up to get out of it, nothing happened. They scrambled up the drainpipe and fell into the room, frightened and out of breath.

"What's the hurry?" asked the clown in surprise. "Is anything after you?"

"Yes, something with a great, big, shining face!" said the teddy. "Ooh, look! It's peeping in at the window!"

Then the clown laughed till the tears ran down his face.

"You sillies!" he cried. "It's only the moon! Fancy being frightened of the moon!"

And sure enough, it was! Teddy did feel silly, but he didn't mind a bit when Belinda kissed him and said he and the clockwork mouse were the bravest of all the toys in the toy cupboard.

"Clown may laugh at you now," she said, "but he wasn't brave enough to come out in the night and rescue me! You and I and the clockwork mouse will always be friends now, won't we?"

And they are. If you look into Mollie's toy cupboard any morning you will see them there, close together – Belinda, the teddy bear and the little clockwork mouse!

Come Back,
Dobbin!

Dobbin was a big wooden horse. He had four legs and they were fastened to a board, and underneath the board were four wheels. Dobbin ran on the wheels whenever Jane or Andrew pushed him.

And then one day Dobbin did a very strange thing. He wriggled and wriggled his legs about on the board, and at last got them all free! He kicked them up into the air, gave a funny little wooden neigh, and galloped off down the garden path!

"Come back, Dobbin!" shouted Jane.

"Come back, Dobbin!" cried Andrew.

But Dobbin didn't come back. He galloped straight out of the gate and down the road. A policeman came round the corner and Dobbin bumped straight into him. Over went the policeman and over went Dobbin – but in a trice the horse was up again, and galloping off on his wooden legs!

"Come back, Dobbin!" yelled the policeman. But Dobbin didn't come back.

He galloped on down the road, enjoying himself very much indeed. But he had left one of his wooden legs behind! It had broken off when he bumped into the policeman. Oh dear!

Dobbin didn't notice. He galloped on quite happily with three legs, neighing every now and again with joy. He ran down a lane and bumped into a fat white goose that was waddling up it. Down went

Dobbin and over went the goose with a hiss and a squawk. She pecked hard at Dobbin, but he galloped on.

"Come back, Dobbin!" squawked the goose. But Dobbin didn't come back. He galloped on down the lane in glee. But he had left his fine hairy tail behind him! The goose had pecked it off!

On he went without a tail and with only three legs. He came to a pigsty and galloped under the gate. A fat pig was in the sty and looked at Dobbin in surprise. He tried to get out of the horse's way, but he couldn't. *Bump*! Into the pig went Dobbin, and over they both went into the mud. In a twinkling Dobbin had picked himself up and off he galloped once more.

"Come back, Dobbin!" grunted the pig. But Dobbin didn't come back. He galloped on, not seeing that he had left two more legs behind him! So now he only had one leg, and it was strange to see him galloping on that. How he managed I don't know, but on he went, galloping happily.

He came to a big street. He galloped down it, dodging the cars and the buses very cleverly. But he didn't see a boy on

a bicycle, and he bumped right into him
with a crash. The boy fell off and all the
apples and eggs in his basket fell out and
rolled over the road. Dear, dear, what a
to-do there was!

A policeman held up the traffic while
the boy picked himself up. Children ran

about picking up the apples. The eggs were all broken. Dobbin lay in the road with all the breath knocked out of him. Then up he got to go galloping off once more. The boy made a grab at him.

"Come back, Dobbin!" he cried. But Dobbin didn't come back. He galloped on. The boy had torn off his fine mane, but Dobbin didn't care about that! On he went on his one leg, with no tail and no mane, galloping happily.

He galloped up a hill. He galloped down again. But the hill was so steep that Dobbin couldn't stop himself at the bottom, and he galloped right into a deep pond there! *Splash*! He was in the water, and because he was wood, he floated.

He floated and he floated. He couldn't get out. The water soaked into him and loosened the glue that stuck his one leg on to his wooden body. The leg fell off and floated away. And then Dobbin's head fell off too, for that was only glued on to his round, wooden body.

"This is the end of me," thought Dobbin, sadly. "Why did I run away? I have lost all my legs – and my tail – and my mane – and

even my body. I was having such a happy time too!"

Jane and Andrew had been most surprised when Dobbin galloped away. "Let's go after him!" cried Jane. So down the road they went, chasing Dobbin. They saw him bump into the policeman, and they found the wooden leg he left behind when he had gone galloping on. Andrew picked it up. Then on they went again, chasing the runaway horse.

Come Back, Dobbin!

They ran down the lane after Dobbin.
They saw him bump into the goose, and
they saw the goose peck his fine tail off.
Jane picked the tail up from the lane
and put it into her pocket. Then down
the lane they ran, chasing the naughty
wooden horse.

They saw Dobbin rush into the pigsty
and bump into the pig. They saw two
more of his legs break off, and they
couldn't help laughing when they
watched the wooden horse gallop away
happily on the one leg that was all he had
left! Andrew picked up the two legs. Now
he had three of Dobbin's legs!

Off the two children went again, chasing
Dobbin. How they stared when they saw
him knock the boy off the bicycle! They
helped to pick up the apples and then they
saw Dobbin's mane lying in the gutter,
where the bicycle boy had thrown it in a
temper. Jane picked it up and put it into
her pocket with the tail she had there.
Then on they went again, quite out of
breath with all their running.

Up the hill they went and down the
other side, just in time to see Dobbin gallop

straight into the pond. They watched him floating there. They couldn't reach him for he was too far out on the pond.

"We will fetch a long stick," said Andrew. "He won't drown, so he will be all right till we come back."

Off they went to get a long stick – and when they came back they saw that poor Dobbin had come apart and was floating about the pond in three pieces! His head was in the middle of the pond, his leg was near by, and his body was the other side of the water. Dear, dear, how strange he looked, all in bits!

Andrew fished about with his stick and caught Dobbin's head. The leg floated near enough for Jane to reach it. Then Andrew ran to the other side of the pond and got the wooden body.

They carried everything home – tail, mane, four legs, body and head. What a sad end to a great adventure! But it wasn't quite the end.

Andrew fetched a pot of glue and a big brush. He and Jane put all the wooden pieces on the floor with the mane and the tail beside them.

"The head and body first," said Andrew, so Jane passed them to him. Andrew glued the head tightly on to the body.

"Now the legs," he said. And one by one with the glue, Andrew stuck on the four legs, underneath the body.

"Now the mane and the tail," said Andrew. And the mane and the tail were stuck on too, in exactly the right places.

"And now, Dobbin, you are going to be nailed on to your wooden board and wheels this time," said Andrew. "You are not going to be glued, for you might wriggle your legs about and get loose again. Nails for you, this time!"

189

Hammer, hammer, hammer! Big nails were knocked hard into Dobbin's wooden legs – and there he was, standing on his board again, a happy little wooden horse, all complete, legs, body, head, mane and tail!

Dobbin wagged his tail. He shook his mane. He shook his legs so that they rattled on the board.

"I'm myself again!" he neighed in delight. "Don't worry, Jane and Andrew! I'll never run away again. One adventure is enough for me. I shall stay safely on my board now and be a good little horse!"

So he did, but none of the dolls will ride him now – just in case he gallops off again!